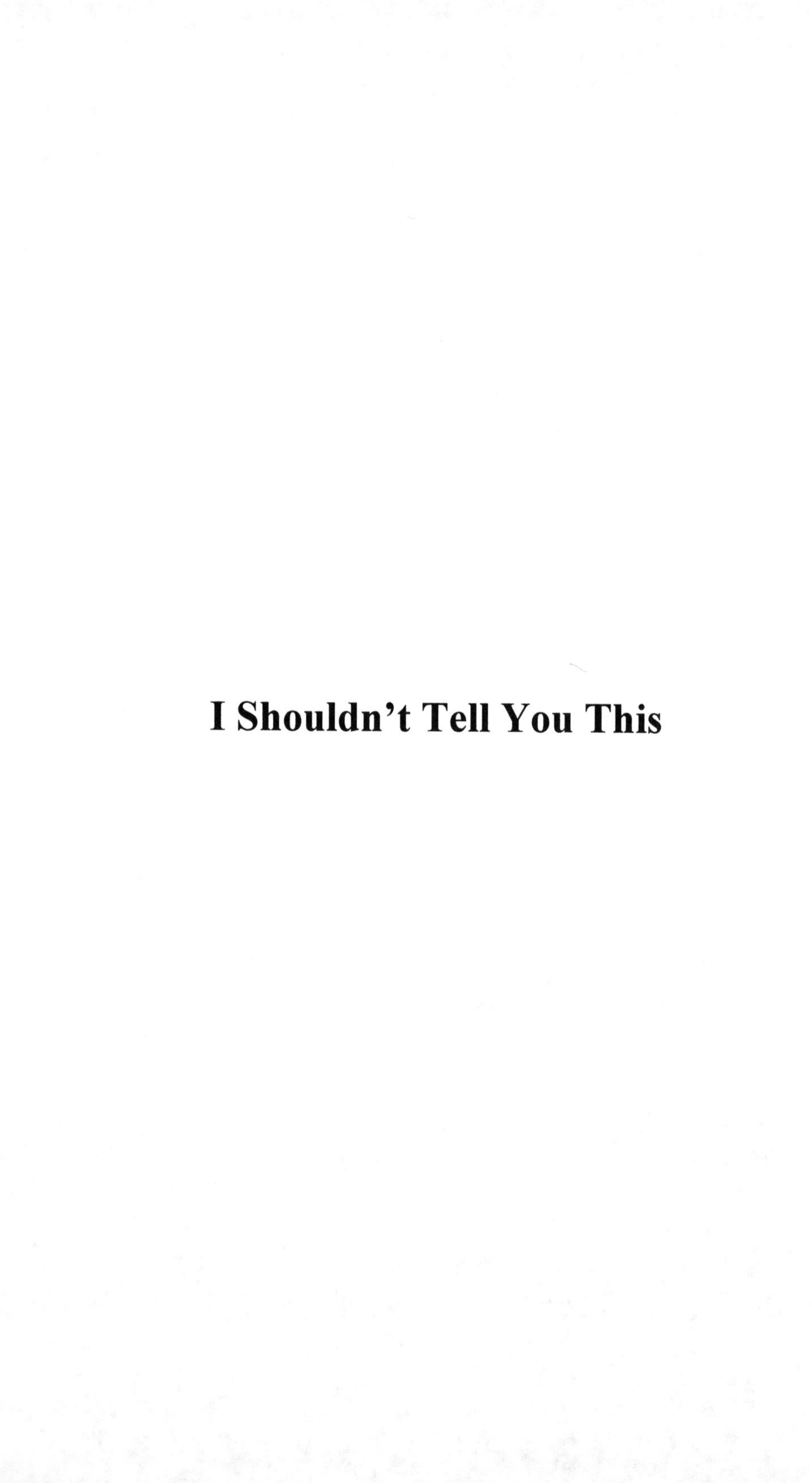

I Shouldn’t Tell You This

I SHOULDN'T TELL YOU THIS

COURTNEY KUKETZ

For Gram- my favorite person even when you don't remember me.

Printed in the United States of America.

For more information, or to book an event, contact :
ishouldnttellyouthis@gmail.com
http://ishouldnttellyouthis.com

Cover design by Brady Weldon

ISBN – 979-8-218-22925-2

I SHOULDN'T TELL YOU THIS

COURTNEY KUKETZ

I.

"Have you seen my passport?" Olivia called out from her disheveled bedroom.

"No. Where are you going?" Olivia's mother asked, poking her head into the bedroom to see her throwing things in every direction.

"Europe," she replied flatly.

"Where in Europe? You can't just tell me a continent!" her mother snapped.

"I don't know for sure yet. I found a cheap flight to Barcelona, and I'll make a plan when I get there."

"What? Is this a joke? When are you leaving?" she asked in a panic.

"I'm leaving tonight. And no, it's not a joke."

Olivia turned away from her mother and went back to focusing on packing. She didn't have her usual packing list, or any type of plan for when she arrived. She was packing light. Strictly essentials. She folded two pairs of jeans, three pairs of shorts, one skirt, one dress, five shirts, sneakers, sandals, a bathing suit, enough underwear for a week, and a few toiletries. One suitcase would suffice. She figured she wouldn't have much time to get settled and unpack anywhere, so there was no point in taking too much. And what did you need to get by, anyway? There were stores everywhere

"Olivia! I think we should talk about this!"

"Talk about what?" Olivia asked, rolling her eyes.

"Where is this coming from? You're not a spontaneous

person. What about that internship?"

"You won't understand."

"Try me!"

"Will you just drive me to the airport in a few hours?"

"Of course I will. That doesn't mean I don't think you're being ridiculous. I wish you'd talk to me about this."

"I have to keep packing. And find my passport. I don't have time to talk!"

Olivia had tried to stay calm and collected with her mother, but she was actually thinking that she was sick of talking. She just needed silence and distance from everyone in her life. What had once been so clear and organized had become too difficult to sustain. No one had ever put any pressure on her to be on a certain life path, but it always felt implied. Even the constant reminders that we never truly know where we will end up in life seemed like a challenge to her. It was always important to Olivia that she be the best; that she prove everyone wrong. And so, when her parents told her she couldn't do something, the voice in her head simply laughed at their lack of faith. Didn't they know by now that she could do anything?

The voice in her head, her conscience, her personal Jiminy Cricket, had gotten this one all wrong, and Olivia had no idea what to do about it.

The voicemail from the head of the internship at the Library of Congress had been brief and dry.

"Ms. Standford, I wanted to thank you for your application. We have taken the time to review your qualifications and potential. Unfortunately, we are not able to offer you an internship at this time. You are welcome to apply again in the fall."

She listened to it over and over again. Why would she have ever felt qualified enough for something like that to begin with?

Her life had started to fall apart, and she was questioning everything she ever believed to be true. She needed to reevaluate her entire life plan. Was she doing as well as she had thought? Was she going to be successful in her career? Was she going to be married? What about children? Did she even really like them? Wouldn't they be a huge burden? Why had she never thought about the more practical side of things before now?

Her thoughts were never-ending, and she was starting to spiral out of control. It was as if her reality was thrown into question in the matter of one thirty-second voicemail.

Olivia knew herself well enough to know she had to stop thinking and get back to the business at hand: finding her passport. She had to be at the airport in two hours.

"You didn't lose it, did you?" her mom asked.

"That's not helpful! No, I didn't lose it!"

She emptied the top drawer of her dresser, thinking maybe it was buried under all of the other things she never touched. There were letters from friends, postcards from every corner of the globe, and birthday cards from people who used to be important to her, but no passport.

"I have it!" her mother yelled from the hallway.

"Why do you have my passport?" Olivia said as she snatched it out of her hand.

"Thanks, Mom. I love you, Mom. You're the best!"

Olivia laughed.

"Thanks, Mom. I'm just stressing out. You know I don't do well with last-minute things. Planning is where I excel."

"I know! That's why I'm so confused about why you are just taking off like this."

"It's uncharacteristic. I get it, really, I do. Just trust me. I need to go."

Her mother nodded and hugged her. The tension in her shoulders melted away for a minute. She felt strangely safe and secure when her mom hugged her and reassured her that there was at least one person in the world who truly loved her, unconditionally. For a minute, she wondered if she needed to get away. Maybe she was exactly where she needed to be. But unconditional love wasn't exempt from disappointment.

Olivia laid her suitcase down in the kitchen and packed her carry-on bag full of snacks, books, a fully charged phone, and comfortable headphones. She was looking forward to the long flight. She knew some people hated to fly, but she loved being above the clouds, looking at things from a bird's-eye view. There was something about knowing she had no control while she was flying that made her feel free. She didn't have to worry; she wasn't responsible for anyone else; departures and arrivals were out of her control, and something about that made it so enticing.

She glanced up and caught her mother staring at her. It may have been in her imagination, but she was sure she saw her chin quiver. There was something sorrowful in her mother's eyes. Olivia tried to ignore it.

"Are you ready?" she asked her mother.

"Let's go!"

Her mother grabbed the keys and headed for the door.

Olivia took one look back, having a sinking feeling that even if the house stayed the same, it would never feel quite like that again. She had always thought traveling abroad would make her worldly and mature. It had to happen eventually. There used to be a fantasy that played out in her mind, time and time again, about spending a semester abroad, finding a tall man with olive skin, bright and welcoming eyes, a perfect smile, and an irresistible accent who would sweep her off her feet. They would have a whirlwind romance for the three months she was out of the country, exchange a tearful goodbye at the airport, and she'd know that for the rest of her life, she would always be able to think about the one that could never be and smile because it was for a little while. Now, romance was the last thing on her mind. She had no room for that in her life. And, of course, her boyfriend might have a thought or two about her running away to Europe to find love.

As they walked out to the driveway, Olivia slung her backpack over one shoulder and grunted a little when she picked up her suitcase.

"You should've asked Dad to carry that for you!"

"I didn't realize it was that heavy. I was packing light. Well I thought I was anyways."

Her mom popped the trunk and Olivia lifted her suitcase, pushed it into the trunk, and tossed her backpack on top of it before slamming the door closed and heading for the front seat. It felt almost like the first day of school. There was anticipation, anxiety, and excitement that gave her the slightest queasy feeling in her stomach, and she was determined to ignore it.

"What terminal are we heading to?"

"Terminal E."

Her mom turned the car on, and immediately Olivia heard the familiar dinging: low fuel!

"Shit! I forgot to fill up earlier."

"Well, let's hurry! Stop at that one before the on-ramp. I don't wanna miss my flight!"

The gas station was only a few miles down the road from their house, so it wasn't much of a time crunch, but as they were nearing the first traffic light, Olivia closed her eyes, trying to will it to stay green. The car lurched to a stop, and her stomach sank. Her mom reached over and rubbed her leg, trying to let her know it would be ok. By the next traffic light, Olivia was no longer silently willing the light to stay green.

"Don't slow down! Keep going!"

Her mom hesitated, and then slammed on the brakes, throwing Olivia's head back against the seat.

"Sorry. I don't want to get a ticket!"

"And I didn't want to get whiplash, yet here we are!"

The two women went silent. There was so much to say, so little time, and neither of them knew where to begin. It was easier to be frustrated with each other. If her daughter wanted to run away to Europe, what was she supposed to do? If her mother was only going to be disappointed in her, what was the point? The green light illuminated the car, and they started moving again. The rhythmic ticking of the turn signal seemed extraordinarily loud while they turned into the gas station. A young man, probably close in age to Olivia, approached the driver's side window with a smile.

"Hi. What can I do for you?"

"Fill it with regular, please."

"Sure thing, just pop the tank open," the young man said as he grabbed the credit card and walked to the pump.

"Think they have guys like that in Europe?"

Olivia started laughing. "I always imagine they'll be better than that!"

"What's wrong with him?

Olivia raised her eyebrows and looked at her mother in disbelief.

"Really? Did you see his teeth?"

"So, he needs a dentist, but that's not the end of the world."

"Shut up! He's coming back!"

"What do you care? His yellow chipped teeth are deal breakers!"

Olivia could feel her face turn red as she glanced up and saw the young man walk towards the car window. The poor guy! His teeth weren't that bad. She wasn't even sure why she'd said that in the first place. Even as she had gotten older, Olivia still couldn't help but be annoyed at the suggestions her mom made when it came to clothing and men. Her mom was always putting her in these awkward situations. It seemed to be her favorite form of entertainment. Her mom smiled and thanked the attendant before turning the car on and heading for the highway.

The mood in the car was way lighter, and as they breezed past road signs and mile markers, Olivia could feel her heart rate quicken and her stomach churning. "No regrets," she reassured herself as she ran her hand over her stomach and took a deep breath.

"You'll call when you get there?"

"Mmmhmm."

"You really don't have a plan?"

"No. Just getting away and seeing a little bit of the world while I have the chance."

They rode in silence for the remaining miles. It felt excruciatingly slow and like the blink of an eye at the same time. She wanted to tell her mom to speed it up a little, but after the stoplight debacle, she thought better of it. There was no point in upsetting her mother right before she took off. Instead, she just got lost in the blurry scenery as they drove down the highway.

The ticking of the turn signal let Olivia know they were close, and then she wished her mother would slow down. She knew she wanted to go, she felt like she had to go, but she wasn't as ready as she was telling herself she was. When the car was pulled over in the drop-off lane, her mother turned to give her a hug and a last-minute moment of reassurance.

"I know you'll be fine. You always are! I hope you enjoy those 'wide-open spaces.' Just don't forget to call!"

"Don't worry, Mom. I know the 'highest stakes.' I'll call a lot; I promise!"

Olivia almost ran into the airport, but as she walked through the doors, she saw her mom still standing there watching her walk away. She hadn't even taken a step toward the car. Olivia smiled and waved at her mom, raising her thumb and index finger to her ear, and mouthing, *I'll call!* before turning and heading to check in at the ticket counter.

The gate was almost empty. Maybe she had overcompensated for her lack of planning by arriving extra early, but she didn't think so. Her flight was scheduled to take off in three hours. That gave her plenty of time to fill a water bottle, use the restroom because no one ever wants to go on a plane, get a snack, peruse the stores, and pick up the latest edition of *Cosmopolitan* to read while she waited for the departure.

It seemed like in the blink of an eye, she'd gone from being alone to being surrounded by sickeningly affectionate couples, screaming children, snoring old men, and someone she was convinced had Ebola.

There were the usual announcements for certain passengers to go to the gate desk before boarding. It always made Olivia so nervous. What did it mean? Were these people not allowed to travel? What if they called her name?

"Would passenger Betty James please report to gate 7?"

Olivia watched as an old woman with a cane meandered over to the desk.

She doesn't look like much of a threat, Olivia thought to herself as she watched the old woman smile and laugh with the young gate agent.

"Would passenger Olivia Standford please report to gate 7?"

Her fear had come true. Why would she be needed at the desk? What was going on? Had she broken some sort of law?

She walked over nervously but put on her best "I'm fine!" face as she got closer to the desk.

"Hi. I'm Olivia Standford. Is there a problem?"

"Ms. Standford, there's not a problem. We just need to confirm your passport information. You booked this flight very last minute. It's a security matter."

Olivia pulled her passport out of her purse and handed it over to the agent. A few minutes of anxiously watching the agent type her information into the computer with the fervor of someone who hated their job, but simultaneously prided themselves on doing it well, was more stressful than she had anticipated.

"You're all set, Ms. Standford. We'll be calling you to board shortly."

"Thank you."

Olivia got her passport back, took a deep breath, and headed back to her seat. She was ready to get on the plane and settle in for a peaceful, quiet, and stress-free flight to Barcelona. She had booked herself a hotel room for the night at a cheap hotel that seemed to be close to the airport, and she figured she would take it from there. Of course, as hard as she tried to let go of the need to plan and prepare for every minute detail of her trip, she couldn't help but worry that she was going to get stranded somewhere.

Deep breaths, Olivia. Deep breaths, she told herself.

She watched couples holding hands and whispering to each other. And she wondered if what those couples were feeling was the same as what she told herself she felt for Cole. They had been dating for a few years, and she was almost ambivalent about him and their relationship. She hadn't even bothered to tell him that she was about to leave the country and head to an undetermined location for an equally undetermined amount of time. That seemed like the type of conversation you should want to have with your significant other. Then again, she knew what his reaction would be, and she didn't want to hear it.

A voice came over the loudspeaker again:

"We will begin boarding flight 456, Boston to Barcelona, shortly. Passengers who have been approved to pre-board may now begin lining up at the gate. Everyone else, please wait for your boarding group to be called."

What felt like an eternity to Olivia passed before she heard the announcement she had been waiting for.

"Passengers in rows 57 to 47 may now begin boarding."

Olivia shot up out of her seat and headed to the line. As her boarding pass was scanned and she walked onto the plane, she couldn't help but worry that she had just made the biggest mistake of her life.

She wasn't built for this sort of adventure. She walked down the aisle and found her seat, praying that she wasn't going to be sitting next to a crying baby or that guy who was clearly dying of Ebola.

*Old lady? She'll probably just sleep the whole time. Jackpot!*she thought to herself as she approached her seat.

"Excuse me, ma'am, I have the window seat next to you."

II.

Betty smiled up at the young woman who would be sitting next to her for the almost eight-hour flight to Barcelona. She was so relieved. This young woman looked so kind. Betty had never flown long distances alone before. And she wasn't sure how she would fare without her usual companion. Every time she was nervous, she remembered what her mother had told her when she was just a child.

"Life is hard, Betty, but the hard stuff is what contains the most precious gems."

And for seventy-three years, those words had not led her astray. In fact, they had encouraged her to try for a better, more exciting life. When a challenge arose, Betty met it head-on, with the determination her mother had passed on to her. Nothing was going to keep her down.

She hadn't expected to be making the trip alone. And she thought about canceling so many times. She had even picked up the phone to call the airline about a refund on more than one occasion. Every time, she would hang up before the phone rang twice. There was no way she could give up on this dream just because unexpected changes made it more challenging. *The hard stuff creates the best moments*. It was her mantra, and she couldn't forget it now.

"Just give me a minute, sweetie. I'm a little slower than I used to be," she said with a smile.

"Take your time. There's no rush," Olivia assured her.

As the two women settled into their seats for the long flight ahead, they were both relieved to not be sitting with someone who would make their trip feel any longer than it was.

The plane started to taxi to the runway, and Betty took a ragged breath. Taking off always made her nervous. The flight attendants went through their usual safety spiel that almost no one listened to. If the plane crashed, they were going to be dead anyway, so there was no point in stressing about what they were supposed to do. Everyone would end up crying, praying, pleading with the universe, and making peace with their imminent ends faster than anyone thought was possible. Time slows when you know it's the end, though.

Betty had figured that out earlier in the year when her Jack had left her. He was the one who had planned the trip. He had held her hand through every takeoff and landing on every flight they had gone on. Now he was gone, and it was a lot harder than she had anticipated. She'd thought she was ready for it. Barcelona was somewhere Jack had always talked about going, and even though Betty didn't care much about the Gothic architecture he was constantly going on about, she felt like she owed it to him to follow through with this trip. And she had to admit, Gaudi's Sagrada Familia church, unfinished or otherwise, was a piece of architecture she wanted to see in person.

The plane began to accelerate down the runway, and Betty closed her eyes and gripped the armrest as tightly as she could. She imagined Jack was sitting next to her, assuring her things would be ok. It wasn't that Olivia made her nervous, but when she opened her eyes to see a young woman, and a perfect stranger, sitting next to her instead of her strong husband, sadness engulfed her.

"Are you ok, ma'am?" the flight attendant asked Betty.

"Yes. Thank you."

"We're about to take off, so just sit tight. Let me know if you need anything. We'll be back with the drink cart when we reach cruising altitude."

Betty peeked over at Olivia and thought she looked so peaceful, listening to music and staring out the window. She couldn't help but think about how lucky that young lady was, and she probably didn't even realize it.

She leaned her head back, closed her eyes, and tried to imagine what Jack would be talking about on the flight to his dream destination. She was sure he would have kept her entertained and excited for the entire trip.

"Do you know the history of Gaudi? No? Oh, honey, you are in for a treat! We are going to get a close-up view of all of his greatest accomplishments."

She could hear his voice that gave away the smile he surely would have been wearing on his lips as he talked about these masterpieces they were headed to see. It was uncanny. He was such a part of her that she could hear his voice even though he hadn't spoken in months. It was the sound she missed most in the world, but it was with her every day. She could hear him every time she walked into a room, every time she got behind the wheel of a car, every time she walked the dog, or when her grandkids came over for a visit. She knew what he would have said to them, and how they would have laughed. It was a sense of humor that far surpassed anyone else's that she came in contact with. He could make the saddest person on the planet crack a smile, and it always seemed effortless.

Humor wasn't considered one of Betty's strong points. She loved to laugh, but she wasn't exactly funny in her own right. She had a quick wit, but a kinder demeanor, so she always second-guessed her jokes, being afraid they were too mean-spirited. Laughter was one of the things she missed most since Jack was gone. That, and having someone to open jars for her. She had been staring at the same jar of pickles for a week, wishing someone could open them for her. She finally understood the plight of single women! No one made them laugh, and they were utterly pickle-less!

Oh, Betty! You're being so old-fashioned! There are gadgets to help open jars now! she thought to herself.

The flight attendant came walking down the aisle taking drink orders.

"Coffee, tea, water, soda, milk, and juice are all complimentary. If you would like to purchase alcohol, we will be back around in a few minutes."

Betty ordered a coffee and passed Olivia the can of soda she had ordered.

The drink cart was quickly followed by food orders.

"Chicken, steak, or pasta are available on tonight's flight. What can I get for you?"

"Oh! How fancy! It's like a flying restaurant!" Betty could barely contain her amusement. "I'll have the chicken, please," she said.

She was starving. She was never able to eat much before a flight. Her nerves wouldn't allow it.

"I'll have the same, thanks," said Olivia.

The two women ate in silence as Olivia left her headphones in and didn't look up. Betty had been hoping she would get to chat with the young stranger sitting next to her, but she thought she should just leave her alone. Not everyone liked to talk the way Betty did. She could just use the time to talk to Jack.

You'd love this meal, Jack.

Her internal conversation with him never really ended.

Suddenly, without warning, her eyes filled with tears.

This was your trip! How can I do this without you? Betty was screaming at him in her mind.

These imagined arguments, and outpourings of rage and frustration, hurt and sorrow, never had the same effect as fighting and crying with him in person did.

One, two, three, inhale, four, five, six, seven, exhale.

"I'm okay. I have to be okay."

III.

This is why I prefer overplanning. I would have ordered a special, low-fat, low-cal meal, Olivia thought to herself.

She wasn't on a diet, nor was she overly concerned with her caloric intake. She just remembered that she had read this article about airline food recently. It got a bad rap. People tended to have really high expectations for meals everywhere, and airplanes were not exempt from those expectations. But this article she'd read explained that you could order different meals, without any extra cost, and they tended to be better. In the article, the author had photographed his food, and it looked more enjoyable than the plain chicken sitting in front of Olivia.

It's pretty hard to mess up chicken! she thought as she cut into the dry piece of meat in front of her.

Olivia noticed the old woman next to her looked teary and desperate for a connection. She tried to shake off the pull she had to even smile at the woman. It seemed cold, but part of the reason she was taking this trip was to experience the silence and not have to engage in unwanted conversation.

She wanted to use the time to center herself and figure out what she was doing wrong. Rarely straying from her path in life had served her well until she'd been turned down for the internship. She'd made it her mission to understand why. What had she done wrong? Why wasn't she good enough? How could she be better?

Unfortunately, it wasn't so cut and dry. There was no real way to be sure why she didn't get the internship. Realistically, she knew it just meant that someone else was a better fit. She had never really thought about the Library of Congress before, and she had no idea what she would have been expected to do. But it would have looked absolutely incredible on a résumé and helped propel her toward her career goals.

Even though she assumed she would never know why she didn't get the internship, she couldn't help but play the possibilities over and over again in her head. It wasn't just her own voice in her head telling her that she didn't deserve the position, and she started to get angry with the other voices. She heard Dr. Jenkins telling her she was smart and talented, and that made her a perfect fit for the internship. That was where the imagined argument started.

How could you set me up like that? Olivia questioned.

Set you up? I was trying to give you a leg up! I thought you'd get it.

You don't need to lie to me! You never liked me, and this was all a game to you!

Olivia was shaking her head and could feel her cheeks flush as she had this imaginary fight with the professor who had recommended her for the internship. She knew he had to have had ulterior motives. No one was ever that nice to her. And although she was a good student, she was far from the best in the class. Something had felt off about the recommendation from the get-go.

Of course, she had always been a quiet student, and she'd barely needed guidance from teachers throughout her academic career, and it rubbed some of them the wrong way.

That's it! I know why you did it. You were trying to knock me down a peg. You think I'm full of myself, overconfident, cocky!

The imagined conversation wasn't getting her anywhere, and Olivia knew it. Sometimes it just felt great to yell at someone without having to say anything. She was far too timid to ever say anything to the professor in real life and to be honest, she wasn't sure if she was being rational about it at all. This man had tried to help her land a great opportunity, but was it more than that?

And then, that day in his office came flooding back to her. She had done well to shut it out of her memory for a while, but she knew it was there. She knew having that interaction would be something she would always struggle with. She knew it was wrong. The problem was, she didn't know who was wrong in that situation. As it all came back to her, she felt the pit in her stomach grow; no matter who was to blame, it didn't sit well with her.

Dr. Jenkins's office hours were Monday and Wednesday afternoons, but Olivia couldn't remember the exact times. Knowing he only allowed students to have their papers reviewed before the due date until that Wednesday, Olivia was cutting it close. She was a good student and considered herself a fairly intelligent person, but there was something about the way Dr. Jenkins looked at her that made Olivia certain that he thought she was the dumbest person he'd ever met.

Walking across campus, trying to talk herself into believing it was going to be a smooth and productive meeting with the surly professor, Olivia wasn't going to turn back. She loved the class, and Dr. Jenkins's dry sense of humor always made her laugh, very quietly while she barely cracked a smile. She tried to focus on the jokes he made and not the looks of disdain he shot her every time she answered a question.

Why does he ask questions if he doesn't want anyone to tell him the answer? she wondered every time.

Olivia walked up the four flights of stairs to the professor's office. The charm and annoyance of attending an old university was the lack of accessibility. Of course, there were elevators, but even if he were located on the tenth floor of the building, she would still rather walk than get into one of those death traps.

At the landing, she took a second to catch her breath before knocking on the door. She double-checked that the cupcakes were not too damaged from the hike upstairs, took a deep breath, and inched closer to the door. She lifted her fist to knock on the door, but she could hear muffled arguing coming from inside the office and froze in her tracks. Should she just come back later? Should she knock? She desperately wanted to have a chance to speak to him about her paper, and hopefully get some useful feedback before the due date. Of course, she also didn't want to deal with him when he was already in a bad mood from the student before her.

Olivia found herself being pulled in two directions. She wanted to be respectful to the professor and the other person in the argument, but she also wanted to be selfish and do what was most useful for her academic career.

Goals, Olivia. You have goals, and you can't let someone else's problems keep you from them.

She knocked gently on the door and cleared her throat to greet the professor, but a young woman barged through the door as Professor Jenkins yelled after her.

"Nicole! Wait! We can work this out! You're so dramatic! God, I hate undergrads!" he said, shaking his head.

Olivia had no idea what to do. It was obvious to her that she had just seen the end of some romantic tryst gone wrong. She didn't know Nicole, but she had heard rumors of someone being involved with Dr. Jenkins. He was a young professor with a chiseled jawline and an air of superiority that was, in some strange way, attractive. It wasn't a surprise to anyone on campus that there would be at least rumors of his involvement with students. But the facts were few and far between, making it one of the more illicit mysteries of the semester.

I guess that mystery is solved! she thought to herself.

Her heart skipped a beat when he noticed her standing in the doorway of his office and greeted her as if nothing had just happened.

"Coffee?"

Olivia just smiled to herself and thought, *I should've known!*

"Miss, can I get you some coffee? A snack?" asked the flight attendant.

IV.

Betty was glad the flight attendant was able to pull Olivia out of her daydream. The girl had seemed to be getting more and more upset.

"You were having quite the argument in your head there, young lady!"

"It was that obvious?"

"Well, when you've been around as long as I have, and you don't have anyone to talk to, you have those arguments a little more frequently yourself."

Olivia just nodded sympathetically at Betty. This old lady had no one to travel with, and it was clear that she wanted to talk to someone. Unfortunately for her, she was seated next to a twenty-year-old woman, who had made it her sole mission not to talk to anyone more than was necessary on her trip.

The two women were separated in age by more than half a century, but Betty had grandchildren, and she was willing to put on her grandma hat to forge a connection with the young woman next to her. But it struck her that she was also faced with a unique opportunity with Olivia. She could finally tell someone her whole story. And since they had hours to kill, and literally no way to escape each other, she figured this was her shot.

"I'm Betty, by the way. What's your name?"

"Olivia."

"It's nice to meet you. You wouldn't mind indulging an old lady in some conversation, would you?"

Of course, Olivia wanted to say no. She wanted to turn her music up, put a pillow over her face, and hide from the talkative woman next to her, but she couldn't turn her back on a lonely old lady. And Betty seemed nice enough.

"Sure. What did you want to talk about?"

"Nothing, in particular, dear," Betty lied.

Olivia was frustrated at the prospect of having to have a conversation in the first place, but realizing that it would be up to her to keep things flowing was an annoyance she could have done without. She wasn't the one who wanted to talk! In her head, Olivia wanted to tell the woman leading the conversation that would have to be her job. But that felt a little too rude, and there was no way she could be disrespectful to a woman as old, or perhaps even older than, her grandmother. So, she took a deep breath and thought of the easiest question in hopes of satisfying this talkative old woman.

"Ok. Have you ever been to Barcelona before?"

"No. This is a first for me. It was originally my husband Jack's dream vacation, but as you see, I'm all alone for this one."

Olivia tried to think quickly, as she recognized that she'd just hit a nerve. This woman's trip was in honor of her dead husband, and once you opened the door for someone to talk about a deceased loved one, there was no way to back out of the conversation without seeming like a complete, utterly insensitive, jackass.

"I'm so sorry. Maybe it will be good to create new memories without him."

"Oh, you're sweet, but I'm never without him."

Betty just sat there and smiled for a minute. It was always bittersweet when she thought about making memories that wouldn't include Jack. It meant she was alive, and her shattered heart was slowly mending. And it also meant that there were things she didn't get to share with him, at least not in the way she had before. Now it was spiritual and emotional. She could feel his spirit with her, but she couldn't see his smile, nor his eyes lighting up with excitement when they stood in front of some incredible monument or piece of artwork.

"What about you? Have you ever been to Barcelona before?"

"No. I just decided it was time for a change of scenery," Olivia said.

"All alone though? No boyfriend or husband? Girlfriend? Friend? No one?" Betty blurted out.

Olivia just laughed. But she wondered how she should answer the question honestly. She did have a boyfriend, but things were complicated, and that was part of the reason she was on the trip in the first place.

She decided to go with complete honesty.

"I have a boyfriend, but things are complicated right now."

"I understand complicated! But you're young, Olivia. How old are you?"

"I'm twenty."

"Oh yeah, definitely young. Rest assured, complicated things have a way of straightening themselves out," Betty explained, not sure if she was trying to comfort Olivia or herself. Maybe it was for both of them.

She knew it was true, and she wanted to be able to pass her knowledge on to someone else, but her own grandchildren wouldn't understand. Olivia was the perfect stand-in. She had no skin in the game, so to speak, and if the plane landed and she walked away believing that Betty was the worst human being alive, well, at least she would never have to see her again.

Before she could get into her own story, Betty needed to know more about Olivia. It would be nice if she could relate to the story a little bit. Honestly, Betty thought all women would be able to relate to her on some level, but she couldn't be too sure. Olivia seemed to be a ball of stress, and she might not be able to see past her current worries enough to even hear what Betty was saying. To make sure she wasn't about to tell a long story that Olivia would tune out for and think was crazy, she had to do a little digging of her own.

"Tell me some more about this complicated boyfriend of yours," Betty said with a smile.

"Things are just weird. I didn't even tell him I was leaving the country, and I know he won't miss me."

"I'm sure he'll miss you! Why wouldn't he want to see your bright blue eyes every chance he had?"

Olivia let out a small laugh, almost out of embarrassment, at the compliment Betty had given her.

“We don't tend to talk too much. We've been dating for a couple of years, but it's almost a matter of convenience at this point. We can go days, sometimes even an entire week without spending time together. I have friends who can't go one day without seeing their boyfriends.”

"Well, do you love him?”

Olivia was taken aback by this frank question. It shouldn't have been hard for her to answer. Either she did, or she didn't. And shouldn't she know the answer to that question? She wasn't lying when she'd said things were complicated with Cole.

"I don't know. I think so, but it's not a fairy-tale kind of love, you know?”

"I know exactly what you mean, dear.”

The two women sat in silence for a moment and let what Olivia had expressed wash over them. She may not have thought it was a big deal, but Betty knew that was a big confession. Most girls in their teens and early twenties would sing their boyfriends' praises, even when they weren't entirely convinced of their feelings.

"Do you remember what it was about him that made you fall for him in the first place?” Betty asked, breaking the silence.

Olivia thought for a minute, shrugged her shoulders, and laughed as she said, “He was cute, I guess.”

Betty laughed.

"I would hope so! But after that, what was it?”

"It might sound crazy, but we are both heavy planners. I need a plan for everything. My life revolves around having one and making sure I reach all of the goals I set for myself. He had similar goals."

"That's honestly a mature reason to be with someone. I have to hand it to you, Olivia. But he has to make you happy! What if you reach all of those goals, and you're miserable?"

"I know."

Olivia thought about that sometimes, but she never believed life was about happiness. It was all about achievement. If you didn't accomplish anything, then your life was pointless! There was no way she was going to have lived and died but leave nothing to show for it. You didn't leave happiness behind. History wouldn't care if she had been happy. Happiness didn't help you reach your goals. Focus and hard work did.

She never thought there was anyone who would say something that made her doubt what she believed to be true. And yet, cruising 35,000 feet above the Atlantic Ocean, happiness, or lack thereof, was all Olivia could think about. Was she happy? Would she look back and wish she had approached life a little differently?

V.

Happy thoughts. It felt a little too close to Peter Pan for Olivia. Happiness might as well be part of a fairy tale. It wasn't that she hadn't had a good childhood. She had never been hungry, every new school year meant a new wardrobe, Christmas stockings were always overflowing, and she never wanted for anything. Generally speaking, life was good.

Having all of the things that should have made her happy hadn't made happiness a reality for her. For almost as long as she could remember, Olivia was only concerned with making sure she could create a similar lifestyle for herself as an adult. She assumed that was what you were supposed to do: take what your parents had given you and improve upon it. She was striving for the American Dream, even if she wasn't sure it was her dream.

How is this old lady making me question things even more than I was before? she thought to herself.

I'm on the right track. My goals are in view. I just need to keep plugging away. Sure, I'm having a bit of a setback right now, but that's to be expected.

Her thoughts were racing.

But she realized the bigger question Betty was trying to focus on was about Cole. How happy was she with Cole? She had never taken much time to think about that. A long international flight without him seemed like a perfect opportunity, though.

When Olivia and Cole met, it hadn't been what anyone would call love at first sight, so much as lust. That was what it always was, though. At least that was what Olivia chose to believe. You couldn't love someone you didn't know, but you could feel a strong attraction to them.

It was freshman-year orientation when Olivia was tapped on her shoulder by a young man, who, by society's definition, was nerdy. Cole was dressed more business casual than most of the other students. His clean-shaven face was outfitted with wireframe glasses and a meek smile.

"Hi! I was wondering if you had a partner for this scavenger hunt happening at the student union later today."

"No, I don't. I'm assuming you don't either?"

"Nope. I'm Cole, by the way. Are you interested in being partners?"

A sense of panic swept over Olivia. She hadn't planned to do anything like that, never mind partnering up with a random guy who'd just walked up to her and asked her, on the spot, to go on this little adventure. She had to think fast, and wasn't college the perfect place for unplanned nights?

"I'm Olivia. I hadn't planned on going. But hanging out with you for the night doesn't seem like a terrible way to spend my night."

Olivia thought she was lucky to have had such a cute guy come up to her, on her first weekend as a college student. She had always preferred slightly nerdy boys, so she knew college would be when she would find the perfect boyfriend. "Nerdy" went from being a negative thing in high school to a compliment in college, but only if you changed the word “nerd” to “academic.” Being smart and focused was a positive characteristic. At least that was what Olivia had hoped to experience in college.

"Awesome! Meet by the juice bar at 7:30?”

"Sounds good! See you then!”

Olivia was beyond excited! What was she going the wear? Part of the scavenger hunt included taking selfies and videos at the different locations around the city, so she had to be both first-date ready, and camera ready. Although both meant she needed to be extra conscious of what she was wearing, they were not necessarily the same.

First-date ready meant something that was the perfect balance between sex appeal and effortlessness, whereas camera ready meant casual and fun, while also cute. After several wardrobe changes, Olivia decided to go casual, even though she knew Cole had been a little more dressed up earlier. She wasn't even sure it was a date to begin with, so she figured there was no reason to go all out, dress up too much, and look like a fool if it didn't end up being a date. Maybe he was just really into scavenger hunts!

She put on her favorite skinny jeans, a turquoise V-neck T-shirt, and white Converse sneakers. If nothing else, she looked like a typical college kid. Of course, she hoped she looked better than a run-of-the-mill college girl to Cole, but she also didn't want to look like she was trying too hard. She didn't have a well-thought-out plan for that type of situation, so she just hoped for the best.

“Olivia! Over here!" Cole yelled to her as she walked through the door.

"Hi!" she said, trying to hide the nervous energy that was surging through her.

"You look nice! You're ready to take pictures when we win!"

She blushed a little as she said, "The pictures are going to look incredible with the two of us holding the first-place prize!"

"Oh definitely!" Cole said.

Cole grabbed the list of clues for places they were expected to find and challenges they had to complete. He and Olivia took a minute to look them over before heading out of the student union. Most of the other students took off running almost immediately. Without even having to talk about it, they both knew reading the clues and having an idea of at least one destination would be the best option.

The way Cole furrowed his brow when he was trying to come up with an answer to a question was something Olivia found adorable. It showed such drive! She was certain he worked hard to make sure he was the best at literally everything he did. With that in mind, she made it her secondary mission to find out just how good he was. But first, they had to win this scavenger hunt!

"It looks like we are going to be taking a lot of videos. You're not camera-shy, are you?" Cole asked.

"Camera-shy, generally shy, call it what you will."

"I'm not a fan of being the focus of pictures and videos, but I hate losing. We're in this to win, right?"

"I don't do losing!" Olivia said.

“Awesome! Let's do this!”

Cole turned back to the list of tasks they had to complete and took charge. The two of them had a lot of work ahead of them. The first task at hand required them to go to a grocery store and ask an associate for the nutrition facts on an inedible product.

"I don't know if this is something I can handle, Cole!”

"I thought you didn't do losing?”

“Using my own words against me? I thought we had a good connection. I guess I was wrong about you!”

They both laughed, realizing these tasks weren't going to be as simple as taking a picture with some random statue. They were going to need to be open to embarrassment if they were going to win the game,

"It'll be a great story of our first date that we can share with our future children.”

"Woah, Liv, you're moving a little fast!”

"Did you call me Liv? And I'm the one moving fast?”

They laughed as they walked towards the nearest grocery store and argued about who would have to talk to the employee. It dawned on them that they should just ask the youngest employee they could find. Either they would think Cole and Olivia were complete morons, or they would be confused and try finding the answer for them. Regardless, they would get their video and could move on to the next item on the agenda.

Racing through the store, Olivia kept her eyes peeled for a teenage employee while Cole looked for something inedible. He wanted it to be something that could be mistaken for something people needed nutrition facts for. "CAT FOOD!" Cole yelled over to Olivia.

She smirked, and thought of the perfect backstory for that, just in case! She always needed to be prepared for things, but social interactions tended to take a little extra planning for her, even when they were just silly games being played.

Cole handed her a can of cat food and took out his phone.

"Excuse me! I'm sorry to bother you, I just need some help."

"Yeah?"

"I can't find the nutrition facts on this can. It's my grandmother's favorite, but the doctor said she needs to watch her cholesterol now. I just want to make sure it's ok for her to keep eating this."

The stock boy looked at her, then the can, and back to Olivia again.

"What does your grandmother make with that?"

"Sandwiches," Olivia said, trying to keep a straight face.

"You realize that's cat food, right? I don't think cholesterol needs to be your grandmother's biggest concern with that."

"I tried to tell her!"

Olivia and Cole ran away laughing. If nothing else, even the start of that night was the funniest experience of her life. Once they were out of the grocery store, they knew the rest of the tasks would be a breeze.

Up next: *Act like a stranger is a celebrity and get an autograph and picture.*

"It's your turn to embarrass yourself!"

"Fine, but where are we going to find someone who will humor me?"

"Maybe if we go to a club or something and find some drunk people?" Olivia suggested.

"Wouldn't it be easier to pretend we're the drunk ones? Like so drunk we think some random person is a movie star whose name you can't remember or something?"

"That might work. Give it a try. I'll have my camera ready."

When they reached the busiest bar in the city, Olivia started pointing frantically at a man walking outside to smoke a cigarette. The man was short, probably 5'6", and had a scruffy beard, a huge nose, and a bit of a potbelly. He wasn't even close to being a dead ringer for the actor. In Olivia's mind, that made him the perfect target for Cole. He seemed like one of those guys who thought they were God's gift to women and believed he was even more attractive than the hottest Hollywood stars. He even winked at Olivia when he saw her pointing at him. She knew it was going to work.

Cole whispered nonsense into Olivia's ear and then headed toward the man.

"Excuse me, sir. You're a famous actor, right? From that space movie with the squirrel? My girlfriend over there doesn't think so. She keeps telling me I'm drunk. I'm not drunk. You're him right?" Cole tried to make his speech as garbled as possible but was ultimately relying on how ridiculous the whole thing was to be enough proof of his intoxication.

"Yeah, man! That's me! What's up?"

"I knew it! Where's that squirrel dude you're always with in the movies?"

The guy just laughed.

"Can I get a picture with you? My friends are never going to believe I met you, and that you lost the squirrel!"

"Sure thing. Your friends will love this picture!"

"Sweet! Ok, ok! Let's get this selfie before I throw up."

"Boot and rally, man! Don't waste the night," the man said as Cole held out his phone.

They took the picture together, and the man started to walk away, laughing when Cole yelled after him.

"Hey! Wait! Can I get an autograph for my girlfriend? She's shy."

And the man signed the napkin Cole had in his pocket. When he was out of sight, Olivia and Cole took off laughing again. Two items down, and so many left to go!

By the end of that night, Olivia and Cole had aching sides from laughing so much, but they just weren't ready to part ways. There was still one item left on their list. They both assumed it was going to be extra challenging and silly.

"Find the statue of the first school mascot, and take a team photo with him!"

"Seriously? After all the crazy things we had to do tonight, this is how it ends? What a flop!" Olivia said.

"Let's make it a fun picture!"

When they got back to campus and found the stereotypical bobcat statue, they froze. What would make a fun, funny, and not-too-embarrassing picture? Everything they suggested felt either boring or way too revealing. Olivia wanted them to be sitting on the bobcat's back, and Cole suggested they do it topless. Olivia was passionately against that idea! They settled on the boring standby of sitting on the bobcat's back. Olivia wrapped her arms tightly around Cole and rested her head on his shoulder for the picture.

"We look like a real couple!" she joked when she looked at the picture Cole had taken.

"That's the goal," he replied quietly.

Getting to the finish line and finding out the results of the hunt seemed like it would mean they would have to go their separate ways. They thought for a minute about not going to the finish line. Neither of them cared too much about the fifty-dollar gift card nor the admiration they assumed they would get if they won. But Olivia had to do things by the book. She'd started this activity, so she had to see it through to the end.

"I don't do losing, remember? Not finishing is the same as losing."

The two of them walked back to the student union to see how they had done.

"Seventh place? Are you kidding me?" Olivia was not pleased.

"Hard to believe, but it was fun. Maybe the people who came in first place didn't have as much fun as we did," Cole suggested.

Cole walked Olivia back to her dorm, and stood at her door, shifting his weight between his feet, and fidgeting nervously. Of course, after having spent the night out on such a memorable adventure, there wasn't much use in being nervous now, but he really liked her. He wanted to tell her that he wasn't happy that they had lost the scavenger hunt because he always wanted to be the best. But that didn't seem like the right thing to say at the end of a first date. Even if it was an unofficial date, he didn't want to mess it up.

"I had a lot of fun with you tonight, Olivia."

"I had fun too!"

"Would you want to go get dinner with me tomorrow?"

"I'd love that! We don't have to do anything crazy to get the food though, do we?"

Cole laughed.

"No. I think we've had our fair share of off-the-wall antics for a while."

"Agreed!"

They did the customary exchange of phone numbers, user names for Snapchat, Instagram, Twitter, and all of the social media platforms they used, to try to guarantee neither of them up and disappeared after the night they had had.

Cole hesitated for a minute. Olivia could hear the keys he was jiggling in his pocket, and she watched as he looked down at the dirt and kicked at the rocks in front of them. He pushed up his glasses that had started to slip down the bridge of his nose. He seemed to be looking for anything that could divert his attention. And then, still kicking at the rocks, he started to lean in close to her.

Olivia's mind was racing in that split second. She had been hoping he would kiss her all night. Was that going to be the moment she had been waiting for? Her heart was pounding faster as Cole put his arm around her, rested his hand on the small of her back, and pulled her closer to him. She closed her eyes, and her anticipation grew as they stood there for what felt like an eternity. Finally, Cole leaned down and gently kissed her on her forehead. Olivia smiled, but couldn't help but feel a tinge of disappointment in the pit of her stomach. She worried that all of his fidgeting and rock-kicking was him trying to find a way out of the impending kiss. What did a kiss on the forehead mean? Did he dislike her? Was she not the type of girl he wanted to kiss? Did she have bad breath? Had she said something to upset him? Once again, her thoughts were racing.

"I'll call you tomorrow," Cole said as he pulled away from her.

"Sounds good."

There was very little that would make Olivia believe she and Cole had experienced the same night. It was more than a tinge of disappointment she felt. She was crushed. When she had a moment to herself, she did the only thing she could think to do: call a friend. A little outside, but still completely biased, perspective on her experience was sure to help her feel a little better about things. It usually did, but that night felt different.

"I love when a guy kisses me on the forehead! There's something about it that makes me feel like he cares. You know?" Jen said.

"No. It feels like something your grandfather would do when you're a little kid! It's not a passionate, 'I want you' kind of kiss," Olivia lamented.

"But he asked you to go out tomorrow!" Jen tried to reassure her.

"Yeah, it's a pity date."

Jen was Olivia's best friend. They had known each other since they were six, so it wasn't surprising that she could almost hear the thoughts running through Olivia's head. And it was almost expected that Rachel could save Olivia from her thoughts.

"That's crazy. He doesn't owe you anything. Why wouldn't he want to spend more time with the most incredible, fun, funny, and intelligent girl on campus?"

Olivia cracked a smile, let out a little sigh, and relented. Even though Jen hadn't met Cole, her argument was strong.

"You're right! I am pretty awesome!" Olivia laughed.

"Remember, sometimes the anticipation is even better than the actual thing. Hold on to that. You can't be disappointed!"

"Like you were with Mike?" Olivia laughed.

"Shut up! We were kids!" Jen said.

Mike had been the boy she had a crush on for most of middle school, and when she finally got to kiss him, things did not go well! At fourteen, few boys had figured out how much tongue was too much. Add in some braces, and it was closer to a murder scene than the PG-13 romantic make-out scene Jen had envisioned. Olivia loved to remind her of that every time either one of them felt lost in love. It could always be a bloody mess!

Thoughts of Cole swirled in her head as she faded off to sleep, unsure of what to make of him and the connection she had hoped they shared.

VI.

"What's going on in that head of yours?" Betty asked.

"Too much!" Olivia answered candidly.

The old woman had drawn her out of her memory and forced her to face the present moment. Olivia realized that even after the first encounter she'd shared with Cole, she wasn't sure if the feelings were real, never mind mutual.

It seemed like Betty had a firm grasp on love, and what it meant to be in love. Olivia figured she had experienced the perfect romance with Jack. She talked more to Jack, who was dead, than Olivia talked to Cole, and he had been right in front of her, completely accessible! She wondered what the secret was.

"Anything I can help you work out? Still thinking about Cole?" Betty asked gently.

"I don't know how much you'll be able to help. I get the impression that you've had a perfect life."

"Far from it!"

Olivia had her doubts. What was far from perfect in this woman's mind was probably a few burnt dinners that her husband didn't eat. Maybe the kids spilled grape juice on the new white carpet. She just seemed like she had to have gone through life without having experienced many doubts or setbacks. Even with her doubts, Olivia smiled at Betty sympathetically, hoping the woman couldn't tell how little faith she had that Betty knew anything but ease and simplicity.

"I bet you met your husband in high school, got married as soon as possible, and lived a blissfully happy life," Olivia blurted out.

"Well, sarcastic attitude aside, you're not entirely wrong. The problem is that things can look perfect, they may even sound perfect at first, but until you hear the whole story, you'll never understand how messy things can be."

Olivia felt like she had been caught red-handed stealing candy from a baby! Why would she be anything but kind to this sweet old lady? The grimace on her face betrayed her, and Betty knew she'd gotten her attention.

"Oh, don't worry about doubting me!" Betty said.

Olivia's usually pale face had turned a shade of deep red, resembling a ripe tomato. It started with her cheeks but moved quickly to her neck and ears. Luckily, she was wearing a sweater that hid the fact that a bright red hue had also spread to her chest. Her eyes were burning. She was incredibly embarrassed. But she just nodded and smiled at Betty.

"I'd love to tell you my story if you feel like hearing about a boring old lady who always had life figured out!" Betty said with a smile.

"I'd love to hear it!"

Olivia's grandparents, both maternal and paternal, had lots of stories, but they weren't exactly relatable. Or maybe she didn't want to relate to her grandparents when it came to love. She would never tell them about her insecurities with Cole, never mind any bigger issues she was facing. To them, she was perfect, and that was how she intended to keep it.

"It's a good thing we have a long way to go, still," Betty said.

Her story was long, and she wanted Olivia to hear all of it. She believed there was a lot to be learned from people who experienced life before you. Faced with telling a long and complicated story made Betty pause to gather her thoughts and decide where to start. She had been waiting for years to tell this story, so you would think she was more than ready to begin, but when it came time to open up, she was temporarily paralyzed by uncertainty.

The beginning, Betty. Start from the beginning, she heard Jack's voice echo in her mind.

She always struggled to tell stories from the right starting point. She would assume people knew things and go right for the "juicier" details. Jack had helped her reel that in a little. But this time she knew the beginning. She knew how Olivia would be able to relate to her story. She needed to tell it from where it all began, fifty-seven years earlier.

"So, you were right. I did meet my husband in high school, and it was all typical teenage, puppy-love kind of stuff to begin with."

With that disclaimer included, Betty started to paint the picture for Olivia. In her mind, it played like a movie she had seen a hundred times. It always started the same way.

After school one day, she had gone down to get a soda, and that's where her fate would change. Betty walked into the soda fountain and noticed a strong, burly-looking young man standing at the counter. She had seen him around before, but that day, when their eyes met and she witnessed an undeniably gorgeous smile form and complete his already perfect appearance, she was hooked.

"I was with my girlfriends, and he was with his guy friends, but that didn't stop us. We split off, and the rest, as they say, is history."

Olivia had figured as much. She'd met a guy when she was very young, and they locked eyes and never looked back.

Betty seemed to understand that. She needed to be a little more specific. She knew that from the outside looking in, things looked like they'd gotten off to a perfect start. They kind of did, though.

"I know! *Perfect*, *easy*, and *lucky* are all words people would use to describe my love life after that. And for a while, there's no denying it was."

She remembered her first date with Harry like it was yesterday.

"When Harry and I left the soda fountain, he asked if I would let him buy me an ice cream the next day. And I couldn't say no! He was the first boy to ever ask me out. I was fifteen and boy was I smitten!"

Now Olivia's mind was really racing!

I thought her husband's name was Jack? What is happening here? Is this old lady senile? Olivia wondered silently.

Betty smiled as she realized the confusion that was creeping over her seatmate. *In good time, dear!* she thought.

She took her time describing Harry and the fun they had on their first date. Times were different, so she had no selfies to show for their adventurous afternoon, but she had the memories. Harry had met her outside of the school gate, taken her by the hand, and walked the three blocks to the soda fountain. He was grinning from ear to ear, recognizing that he was about to have ice cream with the cutest girl in school.

When they arrived, there were no seats at the counter, and Betty noticed a group of her friends sitting in a booth in the back. She was hoping for a little privacy and asked Harry if he would mind taking their ice cream and going for a walk instead. He obliged, and rather than arguing with her about it, he made a suggestion.

"We could go sit in the cemetery."

“That’s a little creepy, don’t you think?”

"Do you believe in ghosts?” Harry teased.

"Umm, maybe,” she answered tentatively, as her heart started to beat more rapidly.

Harry laughed a little more than he probably should have at a girl he was hoping to impress. Fortunately for him, as uncomfortable as she was, Betty joined in with his laughter. It was contagious.

"I’ll be there to protect you. There’s nothing to be afraid of so long as I’m around.”

"Fine. Let’s go to the cemetery, but I swear, if we see any crazy haunted shenanigans, we're leaving."

"You got it,” Harry assured her.

The two of them took their ice cream and walked down a couple of blocks to the cemetery.

They had both walked by a million times before, but only Harry had spent any time in there. It was a favorite hangout spot for the rough-and-tumble crowd he was part of. Olivia shivered as they walked through the gate but chalked it up to a legitimate chill from the ice cream she had just eaten.

"Are you good over there?"

"All good."

"Let me show you my favorite spot in here."

Harry took off running ahead of Betty, who struggled to keep up while wondering what kind of person could have a favorite spot in the cemetery. But Harry's deep brown eyes pulled her in, and she couldn't turn away at that point. Plus, if she left him, she would be alone in the cemetery, and she wasn't prepared for that. Who knew what sort of things happened when you were alone in a place like that.

When Harry finally realized that Betty was lagging far behind him, he stopped to wait for her.

"Are you ready for this?" he asked.

"I doubt it!" Betty retorted.

"Remember that I'm right here to protect you, every step of the way. Just have a little faith."

Faith in a cemetery seemed impossible to argue with. They were surrounded by headstones engraved with crosses and psalms. It was supposed to be hallowed ground if the things the nuns teaching at her elementary school had told her were true. She had her doubts. But at that moment, she felt like the universe, God, and Harry were all there to protect her. She was ready for whatever came her way.

For the first time since they had arrived at the soda fountain, Harry took Betty's hand to lead her somewhere a little more private. Of course, they were alone anyway, so privacy was relative. Any excuse to get a little closer together worked for both of them.

"Harry had pulled me into an open mausoleum and lifted me up onto what I guess was a cement coffin. I sat there and looked at this mysterious rebel with pure wonderment. I wanted to know why he would have any interest in a straitlaced girl like me," Betty explained.

Harry had been curious about her, too. He wanted to know what her real story was. And if she was as perfect as she seemed, he wanted to find a way to be perfect for her.

"What are you thinking, Betty?" Harry asked.

"I'm thinking this cemetery is more romantic than I had anticipated."

"Really?"

Harry stepped closer to her and put his hands on her knees and edged slowly up her thighs. To his surprise, Betty leaned forward, encouraging him to kiss her. Her heart was pounding fast, but something inside of her pushed her toward him.

"I don't know what I was thinking when I did that," she explained to Olivia. "It was as if something possessed me."

Yeah, hormones, Olivia thought to herself. But she just smiled and nodded at Betty, hoping she had more to tell.

Harry recognized what she was doing, and he was torn. He desperately wanted to kiss her. He wanted to do more than that! He had wanted to show her every worldly pleasure he could. And at the same time, he didn't want to scare her away. He retreated from his macho-man attitude and instead thought he would show a more gentle, caring side.

"I didn't understand it. He moved back a little and took my hands in his, and he kissed me gently. It was a nice enough kiss. It was soft and inviting, but it wasn't what I had expected from Harry. I wasn't sure if I had done something wrong, or if it was all a game to him, but I wanted to run away and hide."

I know that feeling, Olivia thought to herself, relieved to have learned that this woman's perfect life had similar hang-ups to her own.

Harry had helped Betty down and held her hand the whole way back to her house.

"It turned out he was just trying to be a gentleman," Betty said.

When they reached Betty's house, Harry bit his lower lip, kicked at the dirt, and struggled to find the words to tell her how much fun he had had that afternoon. His bashful demeanor surprised Betty. She had believed he was tough and self-assured. It turned out he was far from it. Betty smiled softly at him as if to say she knew, and he didn't need to say anything. But Harry couldn't just leave without saying anything at all. He tightened his grasp on her hand, to a point that was almost painful to Betty. She thought about pulling away, but she could see how hard he was trying, and she couldn't hurt his feelings.

"This was great. Can I take you out again this weekend?" Harry finally mustered up the courage to ask.

Betty remembered wondering how that simple question could have made him so nervous. She knew he had taken lots of girls out before her. She had heard stories about his expectations and his refusal to show any sort of affection. There was no way she was possibly making him so nervous. It made no sense.

She would think about that walk home a lot more often than she would the awkward first kiss in a graveyard.

"It was like clockwork. Every day after school, Harry was waiting for me to walk out of the building, and he greeted me with a smile and a quick kiss, before taking my hand and walking me home."

Back to perfect, Olivia thought.

"Do you think the flight attendants will be around again anytime soon? I could certainly use another coffee," Betty said.

"I think you can just push the call button when you need something."

Olivia reached up and pressed the button for Betty, who seemed to get lost in thought as she waited for someone to come by and check on her. Olivia started to think that she didn't need a coffee so much as a moment to relive her story alone. And Olivia welcomed the break. Of course, the story she was listening to was fascinating in its own right, but she couldn't let herself get too lost in someone else's story. She had her own story to replay in her mind.

VII.

Hearing about Betty's kindling romance with Harry sent her right back to the beginning with Cole. That first night was fun and exhilarating, but also confusing and disappointing. It had taken more than a phone call with a close friend to make her feel comfortable and confident enough to go on their second date.

Olivia spent hours obsessing over every last thing they had done while they were together on that scavenger hunt. She was certain that she had made a fool of herself and was little more than entertaining to him. Maybe her faked confidence was completely transparent, and he knew she was a nervous wreck most of the night. She could always think her way into believing she was the worst, most useless, unwanted person on the face of the planet, so it wasn't surprising that she was doing exceedingly well at getting herself to believe that Cole was pitying her, and felt like he had no option other than to ask her out again.

If he was asking me on a pity date, and I didn't show up, that would almost certainly kill his self-esteem, and I couldn't do that to him. I should just go, she thought.

The obligation she felt to follow through with her plans with Cole didn't stop the thoughts that were knocking her down.

If he was attracted to me, he would have made more of a move than that grandfather-style forehead kiss he went for! she told herself.

That was all the proof she needed. When a guy was attracted to you, he made a bigger, more assertive, and intimate move. Whether that was true or not, that was what she believed.

Her guilty conscience pushed Olivia to prepare for the date as if she didn't believe it was a cosmic joke. And despite acknowledging that this was a date, one out of pity or not, she wouldn't allow herself to look too eager. She decided to dress casually, figuring it didn't matter too much.

There was no fancy dinner in her future anyway, so her casual outfit was perfect. Cole had said they wouldn't have to take part in any crazy antics to get their dinner, and he wasn't kidding. Casual was both in his price range and eating style. He had no interest in white tablecloths and tiny entrees.

"So, I was thinking there's this food truck festival we could check out if that's cool with you," Cole said.

"Food trucks? I've never been to one before."

"Are you kidding? It's a low-key adventure, then! We're definitely going!"

It wasn't too far off campus, and the walk gave Cole and Olivia a chance to talk a little more. Their night of zany challenges for the scavenger hunt had given them something to focus on.

"Where are you from that you've managed to never eat at a food truck? I thought they were everywhere!"

"I've seen them before, they just sketch me out. How sanitary is it to eat food cooked in the back of a van?"

"I haven't died, yet! It's well worth the risk."

"If you say so."

Cole had mapped out how he thought they should approach the festival. It stretched up and down a long main road that abutted a grassy field, and he wanted to make sure they saw everything and tried as much as possible. When they got there, Olivia saw a truck that looked appealing to her and suggested they stop there first. Cole's eyes widened, and he let out a shallow breath.

"We can go to that one, but I think we should hit them all in order. Up the right side, and back down on the left. That way we see everything."

"But it's called 'Breakfast Buggy' and it looks like something off of the prairie! And I love breakfast food!"

"A different truck might have something better. And then you'll be disappointed. Let's walk up and down once, reading the menus, and go from there."

Even for Olivia that seemed like a lot of planning and effort. Cole was adamant, though. He knew how they should go about getting food at this festival, and she should just listen to him.

"If you say so," she relented.

They started down the street with the intoxicating aroma of fried food swirling all around them. There was food from all over the world. The lights and sounds from every truck caught their attention as they walked toward them. Music set the ambiance in front of every menu board, and colorful signs made it hard to walk away. Cole was on a mission to make sure they found the perfect meal, while Olivia would have been content with anything he picked.

"Ok. You like breakfast, so we can split a waffle from the Breakfast Buggy. The Tijuana Tacos looked and smelled authentic, so we can share the order of nachos, and then we could finish it off with the ice cream-stuffed cupcake from Caked. Sound good?"

Olivia couldn't believe that he had walked around and decided what they would eat without even asking her. Had she not wanted to go for breakfast first, she was fairly certain that her preferences would have been left out of the equation entirely.

"Yeah. Perfect."

It was, after all, a date he was taking her on because he pitied her, so who was she to have any opinions? Taking whatever he offered her seemed like the best option.

"Ok. You go save us a table, and I'll grab the food. Do you want a drink?"

"Sure. Whatever you get is good."

"Be right back!"

Olivia sat at the first empty picnic table she could find. The festival was pretty crowded, and she was surrounded by what seemed to be the happiest group of people she had ever been around. She hadn't understood that the food truck festival was about a lot more than just the food. People were happy to be out and enjoying the last bit of summer. The weather was perfect, kids could still stay up late, and there was something about the summer that made people feel like eating food outdoors, even the mediocre fried kind, was the most amazing thing they could experience. Maybe it was the memories of family cookouts and endless summer nights from their childhoods that eating outdoors elicited, but she couldn't be sure. Olivia was more interested in bonfires in the fall.

"Sorry that took so long. The lines were crazy!"

"It didn't take long! I was just soaking in all of the festival fun."

"Oh, good. What do you want to start with? Nachos or a waffle?"

"I was going to say we should start with dessert! The ice cream is going to melt!"

Cole tilted his head a little, and Olivia laughed to herself, thinking it was the same head tilt her dog had when he heard an unfamiliar noise.

"I didn't realize I was on a date with such a rebel! I guess we can do that."

His discomfort with the idea was palpable. A person shouldn't eat ice cream before the meal. That just wasn't done!

He cut the cupcake down the middle with such precision that Olivia started to think he was a future surgeon. But they hadn't discussed majors or career goals so for all she knew, maybe he dreamt of being a world-renowned chef!

"I got the vanilla cupcake with chocolate in the middle. I hope that's ok."

"Perfect!"

As they each dug into their half of the cupcake, they realized just how messy this was going to be. It was a hot evening, so that wasn't helping the cause much. Ice cream was melting everywhere, and the cake was quickly saturated in what amounted to ice cream soup!

It was hard not to laugh at the ridiculous situation they found themselves in. Ice cream was dripping down Cole's chin, making him look like a little kid.

Olivia took a napkin, reached across the table, and wiped his chin for him. Her half smile and bashful eye contact made him laugh. It was completely embarrassing to have someone you were on a date with clean your face off like she was your mother, but at the same time, he loved the glimpse of her nurturing side.

"Thanks. I'm such a slob!"

"Imagine the mess if we had saved that for the end!"

Cole bit his bottom lip, and realized his plan and need for an exact order of things would have ended in disaster when it came to their dessert.

"What should we try next? Nachos?"

"Yes! Who says no to nachos?"

As they hovered over the plate of chips, they seemed to fall back into the banter they had started the night before on the scavenger hunt. Maybe they needed embarrassing things to happen if they were going to enjoy each other's company.

"Oooh! These are spicy! There are a ton of jalapeños! Did you remember to get drinks?"

Cole froze! He had messed up yet again. He completely forgot about the drinks. He scrunched his face in embarrassment.

"Sorry! I'll go get some now."

"No, let me. I need to stretch my legs."

Olivia got up and headed right for the lemonade stand she had been eyeing from the time they arrived. She was a sucker for fresh-squeezed lemonade, and it was so hard to find!

"Hi! Can I have two lemonades?"

When the girl behind the counter turned to get her drinks, Olivia noticed the candy on the shelf. She had no idea if Cole was going to like it or not, but she decided she had to bring candy back as well.

"Can I get a pack of those Lemonhead candies, too please?"

She put the candy in her pocket and grabbed straws, half a container of napkins, and the drinks. She walked back to Cole, smiling and proud of what she hoped would go over well with him.

When she reached the table, she plopped the napkins in front of him without so much as a word before handing him his lemonade.

"I love everything lemon. I hope that's ok."

"Yeah, but did you have to cut down a tree to get all of these napkins or what?"

"Hey! You might decide to cover yourself in food again! I didn't want to take any chances," she said with a smile.

"Fair enough."

While Olivia went to get the drinks, Cole had taken all of the jalapeños off of the plate. He didn't want her to hate them. Plus, it was her first experience at a food truck and they'd already had an ice cream mishap. If she hated the nachos, there'd be no convincing her to go back to one again.

It was hard to mess up nachos, but Olivia had seen it done before. These nachos were really good! She couldn't figure out if it was the addition of a barbeque sauce or the chicken that made them so good. Then again, she thought it may have been the onions. That was the thing about nachos, it was impossible to know for sure what made them so good. Everyone could make a different type of nacho that was incredible, but if you took one topping away, it would be terrible.

"I've never had nachos like that before. Barbeque sauce sounded so out of place, but now I think I want it on all of my nachos!" Olivia said.

"I wouldn't go that far. Imagine putting it on the weird liquid-cheese nachos you get at a sporting event. I feel like that would be a disaster!"

"Don't judge it before you try it!"

"You can try it first."

"I would almost be willing to bet money that we could go to a store, buy some of that premade, jarred queso, put that on top of some chips with sliced onions, jalapeños, scallions, shredded chicken breast, and then drizzle the barbeque over the whole thing, and it would be your new favorite food!"

One thing Olivia felt didn't need to be followed exactly was a recipe. She figured if you put things together that seemed to complement each other, only good things would happen. That wasn't really true, and she had found that out when she tried the craziest concoctions she could come up with when she started cooking, but more often than not, good things happened and that was enough reason for her to keep thinking that way about cooking. Cole didn't like that. He had grown up watching his mother cook from a cookbook every night. She used one even when it was a recipe she had made once a week for decades. In their household, you couldn't be too careful with a recipe. Food wasn't to be used as an experiment. Cole was never going to see it her way when it came to food.

"I don't think so! That would be a soggy mess!"

"Like that cupcake you had?" Olivia retorted.

"I'm never going to live that down, am I?"

"Nope. Get used to it."

"Anything that means I get to hear you laugh is something I can live with."

Olivia was caught off guard by that response. She was flattered, but one of her favorite things to do was banter back and forth with someone. She felt like that was when her personality could shine the brightest. It took a minute for her to remember that this was a date, and he was being flirty. And that was what she should have wanted from him. She looked down and smiled, not sure there was anything she could say back to that.

"Ok! What's next up on our culinary adventure?"

"I got us the ultimate waffle!"

"What makes it ultimate? Is that just what the menu calls it, or do you know that it's ultimate?"

Cole did the little dog head tilt again, making Olivia laugh.

"Can't it be both?"

"No! Have you had this waffle before?"

"No, but listen to what's on it!"

He went through and retold the description from the menu.

"It's salty and sweet because there are bacon pieces and chocolate chips baked into the batter, and then it is topped with sliced strawberries and covered in powdered sugar. That sounds pretty ultimate to me!"

Olivia laughed at his enthusiasm, and she had to admit, it sounded pretty incredible.

"Wait, you think it's ok to put things in waffle batter, but you think I'm crazy for even imagining putting barbeque sauce on liquid cheese-style nachos? What a food snob!"

Cole shrugged, poured some syrup over the waffle, and dug in.

"I can just eat this by myself then," he said with his mouth full of the sugary breakfast creation that made Olivia's mouth water.

She laughed and grabbed her own fork to make sure he didn't eat the whole thing. It was undeniably the best waffle either of them had ever had. The crisp outside was counteracted by the fluffiness and melted chocolate in the middle. When they happened upon a crispy bit of bacon, it was just an added bonus.

"You win. This is the ultimate waffle! It doesn't matter why you called it that."

"I told you last night, I don't do losing, so you should get used to it."

Cole reached over the picnic table and took her hand. Olivia's heart quickened as she hoped for more than a forehead kiss. She imagined the passion that had been boiling inside coming out as sparks between the two of them.

He smiled at her and asked if she was ready. She assumed he meant ready to end the date and go home. Even if she had wanted to object, she couldn't find the words.

"Yeah, let's go."

He stood up from the table and walked over to her, making sure to take her hand again as they headed out of the festival.

"That was a lot of fun. Thanks for introducing me to food trucks!"

"Of course."

The pair walked in silence for a while and the uncertainty of where it was all headed weighed heavily on Olivia. Cole wanted to have a food truck festival game plan, but she wanted a life plan! She thought there was a possibility that Cole could be part of that plan, but she wasn't sure just yet. It was only a first date, after all. She was getting ahead of herself, and the voice in her head was screaming at her to tap the brakes.

"Come this way!" Cole said as he pulled her down a dark alleyway.

"What are you doing?"

"This just looks more private," he said.

When they were far enough into the alley that they couldn't see the street lights anymore, Cole turned toward Olivia and pushed her against the wall behind them. He grabbed her wrists and held them above her head in one hand while slowly tilting her face up toward him with the other. He looked into her eyes with a passion and intensity she had never experienced before. He was in complete control, and there was nothing Olivia could do about it. She couldn't even bring herself to blink out of fear it was all a dream. Slowly, he got closer to her, in a way she hadn't thought was possible. She could feel the rhythm of his heartbeat as their breathing fell into sync. Olivia closed her eyes and hoped he was going to relieve her of the anticipation and desire that had been building inside of her. Cole leaned down and brushed his lips against hers. It was a soft, playful kiss at first. His tongue found hers and pulled forth a longing she was unaware she had. Olivia could have stayed in that moment forever, their lips fused as one, and their tongues dancing the tango, but reality called when a group of boys rode past them on bikes, and let out a cheer of encouragement for Cole.

Cole backed away from her for a moment, and they both laughed awkwardly as if they were seeing each other in the light of day for the first time. Both flushed and hesitantly optimistic, it seemed like a good time to get out of the alley.

"You taste like lemons," Cole said as they started to walk back to campus.

"Oh, I forgot! I bought these Lemonheads for us. I love them! Want one?"

"I was wondering what your secret was to being so sweet! I'd love one, I'm just afraid it will make me want to kiss you again."

"And that's a bad thing?"

VIII.

"Here's your coffee, ma'am. Do you need anything else right now?"

Betty tapped Olivia gently on the shoulder and asked how she was doing. She could see the young woman's face was flushed, so her thoughts were probably on the more intense side of things.

"I'm good. You got your coffee?"

"I did. Isn't it amazing that they can make a fresh cup of coffee while flying so far above the earth? I'll never understand how things like that are possible."

"It's pretty incredible."

"So, where was I in my story? Oh yes. The good days with Harry."

"Your perfect romance!" Olivia blurted out with a little laugh.

"Nothing stays perfect, don't worry."

Olivia just raised her eyebrows and nodded, waiting to see what imperfection was to Betty.

She started to recount the days after school when Harry would greet her and walk her home, so she didn't have to be alone. But there was something about Harry that had changed in the short time they had been seeing each other. When they met, he was a tough guy whom no one would dare upset, but he also had a really sweet side to him, the one that pulled back and didn't go too fast for Betty. That was something she loved and hated about him. It always made her question if he was even attracted to her.

What kind of man didn't want more? And she knew, if he tried to push for more, it wouldn't have taken much for her to give in.

Everyone looked at Betty and saw this prim and proper young lady, who would never disobey her parents, never mind go against the values that had been instilled in her, both at home and in church. Her parents weren't too happy when they noticed she was coming home holding hands with a boy, so she could only imagine the fallout when they realized she was kissing him! The scandal it would create for her family was more than she could bear to think of, yet at the same time, it excited her. She loved the feeling of rebellion and danger Harry let her feel without ever having to be in any danger. The danger was attractive. She was turned on by the thought of unknown surprises that could come her way at any moment.

The uncertainty that wasn't a turn-on for her was introducing Harry to her family.

"I think I should meet your dad," Harry said.

"Why? You won't like each other."

"It feels like that's the right thing to do. I need to meet the people who raised such an amazing person, and I need your dad to trust me."

"I'll think about it."

"No, Betty. This isn't something you can just sweep under the rug. I'm serious!"

Seeing him demand to meet her family was so confusing to her. Yes, she liked it because it meant he was serious about her. But also, how serious was she about him? She had no interest in meeting his friends, never mind his family. What did that say about her?

Betty leaned in to kiss Harry goodbye, and walked into her house, full of uncertainty and confusion. She had no idea what she was going to do, even though the answer seemed to be out of her control.

The next day, when she walked out of school and was met with a hug and a smiling face, she had an answer for Harry,

"Ok, I’ve decided. You can meet my family. But there are some rules.”

"Yeah, sure, anything!” Harry, unable to hide the excitement in his voice, said.

As they walked home, Betty listed the rules for him,

"Rule number one, be on time. Two, don’t smoke or wear anything you have smoked in. Three, don’t drink before you come over. Four, no physical contact that goes beyond hand-holding. Five, don’t talk about hanging out at the cemetery. And the last rule, don’t try to joke with my dad, it will just make him angry.”

"No problem. I can follow those rules.”

“Great, so dinner starts at 5:30. What day do you want to come?”

"Tomorrow?”

"Ok, it’s a plan.”

Betty stood on her toes and kissed Harry as if it would be the last time she ever kissed anyone. In her mind, they were about to go to battle tomorrow, so she needed to have her fun while she could. It wasn't going to go over well. There would be no more after-school jaunts to the graveyard to hide and make out in a mausoleum.

Harry didn't meet Betty after school the next day, so she started to think he had changed his mind about meeting her family. She had been dreading it, but it was a lonely walk home, and she was hurt that he didn't even have the common courtesy to tell her he had changed his mind. Standing her up, on any occasion, was uncalled for and hurtful. To do it after having made a big deal about having dinner with her parents was unforgivable.

The angry and sullen walk home left her with ample time to decide what she was going to say to him if he dared to speak to her again. She didn't even want him to be nice all the time, she just wanted him to show up when he said he was going to so she wasn't embarrassed. She felt certain that she would be met with accusations and ridicule when dinnertime rolled around and her boyfriend didn't show up after she had already told her parents to expect him.

Her eyes brimmed with tears, out of both anger and disappointment. There was nothing she could do to change the situation, and being stuck with the hurt Harry had thrown at her wasn't something she wanted to settle for. She thought about heading to the cemetery to see if he was hiding there with his friends, but she didn't think it was her responsibility to go find him. He was supposed to show up for her.

From her bedroom, she heard the doorbell ring. She had been lying face down in her bed, trying to brace herself for an even more uncomfortable dinner than she had originally envisioned, but a jolt of hope ran through her when she heard the bell.

"Betty, your dinner guest is here," her mother called from the living room

Betty wiped her face, looked in the mirror to make sure she didn't look too puffy from all of the crying she had done since she got back from school, straightened her hair, and walked into the living room with a smile on her face.

As she walked into the room, she saw Harry standing in front of her mother and holding a bouquet of daffodils. The yellow flowers seemed to light up his freshly shaven face. As soon as she saw him, she forgot that only minutes earlier she had been ready to end things with him, and never see him again.

"Hi! I'm so glad you could make it!" she gushed as she walked over to give him a quick hug.

"Aren't you going to introduce me to this handsome man?" her mother asked.

"Of course. Mom, this is Harry. He's become a very important person in my life recently."

Harry was beaming as her mother reached out to shake his hand.

"It's a pleasure to officially meet the young man who has been taking up so much of Betty's time."

"The pleasure is all mine, Mrs. Walker."

Everything was smooth sailing at that point. Harry had made last-minute stops at both the florist and the barbershop. He may have been perceived as a tough guy, but his mother had taught him manners that included never going to dinner at someone else's home empty-handed. He wasn't much of a cook, and bringing alcohol seemed risky, so he'd settled for flowers. Betty had told him how much she loved daffodils one afternoon when they were walking through the cemetery. She always took note of the well-tended gravesites and hoped that when she died, someone would care enough to leave her flowers.

"I'd rather give you flowers while you're here to enjoy them," Harry had told her.

Flowers were a simple and tired cliché, even all those years ago, but that didn't stop Harry. He wanted every day to be as perfect as possible for Betty. So, he'd started to bring her flowers once a week when he met her after school. She loved them all. Some days it was roses, others he brought tulips, daisies, begonias, or sunflowers. She never knew what to expect, and that made it a little more exciting. Regardless of what type of flower he brought her, she was never disappointed. But that day, he brought the daffodils for her mother, and Betty had to admit, she felt a tinge of jealousy! She remembered thinking that he should have brought flowers for each of them, but she shook that thought off almost as quickly as it had appeared. She was over the moon that he had shown up, on time, and with impeccable manners, to meet her family.

As it got closer to 5:30, Betty's father arrived home, took his work boots off, and headed straight for the bathroom to shower and get ready for dinner. He didn't even look in Harry's direction. While her mother was in the kitchen finishing dinner, Harry pulled Betty aside.

"Your parents hate me! This was a mistake!" he said, panicked.

"Will you calm down? No one hates you. You haven't even met my father yet, and my mom loves the flowers. You're doing fine," she said, hoping to reassure him.

"Your dad didn't even look at me. He's so mad that I'm here to ruin his dinner and steal his daughter at the same time!"

"Steal me? I can't be stolen. But if you say something like that, he might punch you, but that's only if I don't do it first!"

Harry nodded and tried to get a grip. He knew he was acting a little unhinged, but he needed to make a good impression that night. Luckily, the smell of roast chicken and garlic wafted through the air, letting everyone know dinner was almost ready to be served. The clanging noises from the kitchen were a welcome sound to the nervous and hungry couple. Food was a great distraction. Betty took Harry by the hand and led him into the dining room, having him take a seat next to her, and as far away from her father as the small table would allow.

Her mother carried the chicken in and placed it in the center of the table. The skin had a perfect golden-brown hue, and the crispy cracking sound it made when she sliced through it made everyone know they were going to enjoy dinner that night. Perfectly mashed potatoes, followed by broccoli and dinner rolls, were passed around the table before everyone was given a chance to take a slice of the long-awaited chicken. It wasn't that chicken was a difficult dish to make, but there was something special about her mom's roast chicken. It was a recipe that took Betty decades to perfect on her own.

Every time Betty's father so much as looked in Harry's direction, Harry would fidget in his seat, making dinner feel more like a criminal interrogation than a social gathering. Betty was so confused. Why would Harry be so nervous when this meeting was exactly what he had demanded of her? She tried to give him reassuring glances throughout the meal, but it seemed to make him worse. It was like he didn't want her parents to know they even spoke to each other!

"All right, Harry! What are you hiding?"

"Excuse me, sir? Nothing! I swear!"

"Well then, why are you acting so squirrelly over there? I get the impression that you are hiding some big government secret, or a murder plot!" Betty's father said, winking at her.

"Uhm, no! I'm, well, I'm..."

"You're what? Spit it out!"

Betty was having a hard time keeping a straight face watching her father make Harry squirm so much.

"I'm here to tell you that I really care about your daughter."

"That's it? You just care? Good to know."

"A lot!"

Betty's father laughed, and Betty couldn't help but join in. He had certainly scared Harry, and it was incredible.

Harry smiled and his face turned a deep shade of red. He was so embarrassed. Why had he been so afraid? Betty's parents were nice, and the dinner was relaxed and informal. There was no reason for him to have been freaking out so much.

Betty helped her mother clear the table and get the dessert. This was, after all, a special occasion. It wasn't every day that Betty brought a boy home for dinner. While they were in the kitchen, Harry was left alone with her father, and he was finally starting to relax a little. It hadn't been the stressful night he had anticipated.

"Are you finished with school? You seem older than Betty."

"I'm seventeen. And I don't go to school anymore."

"Don't go because you graduated and got a job, or don't go because you are a loser?"

Harry's heart was racing. No, he hadn't graduated, but was he a loser? He thought that this was going to be the end of things with Betty.

"Well, uhm, I, no."

"No? No what?"

It felt like Betty's father, who was across the table from him, was towering over Harry, who started to feel like shrinking away was his best option. If only that were an actual possibility.

"School wasn't for me," he said with a ragged, nervous shake to his voice.

"Not for you? Can you read? Are you slow?"

The questions were coming at him faster and with greater intensity than he was prepared for. The interrogation seemed to last forever, and he started to wonder when Betty was going to come back with the dessert.

"I'm not slow. And yes, I can read."

"Do you have a job?"

"No."

Harry looked down at the table, feeling ashamed, knowing he wasn't good enough for a girl as amazing as Betty.

"Do you love her?" her father asked more gently.

"More than I can even explain!"

"Good. Now you need to get a job. I can't let my daughter stay with some guy who isn't going to provide her with a decent life. She's smart. She'll make her way with or without you. But I can't let you hold her back."

"I understand. I'm trying, sir. I want to be better because of her!"

Her father just nodded and looked up as Betty walked in carrying a pie and dessert plates. She felt like the air in the room had changed while she was in the kitchen. Her heart raced a little faster as she looked between her father and Harry. The noticeable tension in Harry's shoulders was a dead giveaway. Her father had changed his tune about him, and she had no idea why. What could have happened in the five minutes it took her to get dessert in the next room? The forced smile on her face was met with a similar expression on Harry's face. Her mother came floating into the room without a care in the world, with a hot pot of coffee, and cups for each of them. Her father acted as if nothing had transpired while she was in the kitchen, smiled up at his wife, and cut into the pie.

Harry devoured the piece of pie he was given in what seemed like one bite and gulped the scalding-hot coffee down as quickly as possible.

"Wow! You finished so quickly! Want more?" her mother asked, excited to see someone enjoy her dessert so much they couldn't contain themselves.

"Oh, it was delicious, but I'm stuffed! And I have to get going, anyway. My mother is expecting me home soon," Harry lied.

"Well, I'm glad you enjoyed it. Take some home with you! We'll never eat this whole pie!"

"Speak for yourself!" her father chimed in.

Harry wasn't sure what to do. Take the pie and be polite to Betty's mother, or leave it out of respect for her father.

"Shut up, Jim. The boy can have the pie! I insist!" her mother asserted, saving Harry from having to choose for himself.

"Thank you! It really is delicious."

With his pie in hand, Harry headed for the door. When he was met by Betty's father, he was taken aback. He had assumed Betty would walk him out.

"Look, kid. You need a job, but you seem like a nice enough young man. Be at this address tomorrow morning at 7:30. Be ready to work."

And he slipped a piece of paper with a street address into Harry's hand.

"What was that all about?" Betty asked, running up behind him in the walkway.

Harry shook his head in disbelief. He wasn't sure what to make of her dad, but it seemed to be good.

"I think your dad just offered me a job."

He shrugged and pulled Betty in close to him. Once she was pressed against his chest, their hearts beating as one, he let out a sigh of relief.

"That was a stressful dinner!"

"I told you there was no reason to put yourself through that," Betty reminded him.

"You're so smart. I should listen to you more often."

"Yeah, you should!"

Harry looked at Betty, tilting his head to get a better view of her before reaching down and lifting her chin to pull her face closer to his. Just before he leaned in to kiss her, he stopped himself, looked deep into her eyes, and said, "I told your dad that I care for you, but it's so much more than that. I love you, Betty."

And after a quick glance at the window overlooking the walkway, he kissed her forehead gently and turned to walk away. When he reached the end of the walkway, he turned and said, "To be continued."

Betty was speechless. Love? Love was a strong word. What did she think of him? It was fun to have someone bring her flowers and walk her home from school. Having him at dinner had made the meal a little more entertaining than usual. But love?

Betty went to bed with her mind on fire. She knew she was supposed to find the right guy to marry and have a family with. She would be old enough soon, and that would be expected. How would she ever know if she had found the right person, though? She liked Harry, but she liked a lot of people. Was having affection for someone reason enough to spend a lifetime with them? Being rough around the edges was fun, but was it practical? And it wasn't like she had many opportunities to meet people, so was it possible that he was the best she was ever going to find?

The racing thoughts kept her awake for the better part of the night. All the most adult and important choices of her life came to the surface for her, and there was no escaping them. She hoped her puffy eyes wouldn't betray her when she went to school in the morning. She had a sinking feeling that everyone would be able to tell that she had just had one of the most difficult nights of her life, and her entire perspective on life was shifting.

When she walked into the building the next morning, she was surrounded by people her age, all paired off and living a blissful existence in coupledom. They were happy and were all probably very comfortably and confidently in love. Marriage was on the horizon for all of them, and Betty was the only one who wasn't so sure about her prospects.

"Do you think you're going to marry Phil?" she asked her friend when they met at their lockers.

"Marry? We're in high school! No time soon!"

"But eventually?"

"I mean, I've thought about it. I want to get away from my parents as soon as possible!"

"Would you say probably?"

"Jesus, Betty! What has gotten into you?"

She looked down at her shoes, avoiding any further eye contact.

"Forget it. It doesn't matter."

The rest of that day was a bit of a blur as she tried to convince herself that there was no reason to make a life-altering decision regarding her relationship with Harry right now. She was able to block the thoughts out for a little while during some of her classes, but when the final bell rang, and she walked out of the school, she was greeted by Harry and the worries came flooding back to her.

"Why don't you look happy to see me? Everything ok?"

Betty smiled and wrapped her arms around Harry.

"Better now that you're here. It's just been a long day."

"Long day? Me too! Want to go relieve some stress? We can go visit the cemetery."

That had become an entirely transparent code for something far more explicit than visiting graves. And Betty was more than happy to find a way to relieve some of her stress, but that almost seemed counterintuitive. Wouldn't greater physical intimacy with Harry make it impossible to stop thinking about him? But she started to think that the fact that she couldn't say no, that she felt a magnetic pull to him and their macabre make-out spot, told her exactly what she needed to know. Maybe it was love.

Once they reached the gates of the cemetery, Harry took charge. He stayed steps in front of Betty, but never let go of her hand. Gentle tugs forward encouraged her to move faster, as if she wasn't already rushing and out of breath. As they entered the mausoleum, Harry grabbed her by her waist, and in one swift motion, lifted her onto the cement coffin. They were both speechless as he climbed up to be closer to her. He pushed her hair out of her eyes and leaned her back. He climbed on top of her, and as their lips met, he slid his tongue softly into her mouth. His tender caress of her tongue sent warm, electric feelings running through Betty. She let out a quiet moan as her heart beat faster. Harry moved his hands under her top. The movement of his fingers, tracing slow circles at first, followed by tight pinching, and back to slow circles again, was like nothing Betty had felt before. She moaned louder into his kiss, and slowly bent her knees, offering an unspoken invitation for Harry to move closer before wrapping her legs tightly around his waist. He pulled away from her kiss, and took her shirt off, letting it fall to the ground as he started to kiss her neck, moving slowly down, tracing her collarbone with his tongue. With every move he made, Betty tried to pull him closer to her. As he reached her waist, he paused. Betty let out a disappointed groan.

"Please," she said.

"Are you sure?" he asked quietly as he reached for the waist of her pants.

"Mmm-hmm," she said, digging her nails into his back.

Harry pulled at the buttons on her pants with one hand while sliding the other inside. Just the graze of his fingertips made Betty feel like her heart was going to explode and it would be the most amazing feeling in the world. Harry couldn't contain his desire any longer and quickly tore his clothes off. Betty had never seen a naked man before, and looking at Harry made her breath catch in her throat. She could only imagine what he was going to do. She reached out and touched him, surprised to see him shiver at her touch. Her hand moved away from him in shock.

"I'm sorry," she whispered.

"No. Don't stop," he said breathlessly.

He guided her hand, stroking slowly at first. Without a word, he pushed to lay her down and moved back between her legs. She closed her eyes and took a deep breath. She wanted to feel him inside of her, filling an unknown void. He kissed her again as he thrust himself into her. There was a moment of pain and she gasped before lifting her hips, taking more of him. Harry moaned in her ear as he moved rhythmically inside of her.

Betty let out a bloodcurdling scream.

Harry panicked. What was she screaming about?

"What's wrong? Did I hurt you?"

"Get off! Get off of me!"

He had thought they were enjoying themselves. Suddenly it occurred to him that he was enjoying himself, and being with her felt amazing, but maybe it wasn't good for her. He pulled out, got off of her, helped her to her feet, and picked up her clothes. She ran out of the mausoleum without even buttoning her pants. Harry grabbed his clothes and ran out after her.

"Betty! Wait! What did I do?"

She stood there, completely out of breath and as white as a ghost.

"Nothing! It wasn't you. A huge spider was crawling up my leg!"

They both burst out laughing.

Betty got closer to Harry and wrapped her arms around him.

"It felt incredible. You are incredible. Maybe we can try again in a real bed?"

He kissed her deeply, and then reluctantly pulled away.

"Are you sure we need a bed? We can go behind that tree and pick up where we left off."

Betty slapped his arm and the two of them headed out of the cemetery.

Weeks went by, and things fell into a routine again. There were no more awkward encounters with family members, although Harry had become a regular at dinner, and the cemetery was only visited for long walks together. They decided their rendezvous in the mausoleum hadn't been the best idea.

Harry loved his job with Betty's father, and he excelled at it. In no time at all, he was working his way up the ranks at the factory, and saving every penny he could. At the end of Betty's school year, Harry surprised her with a dozen roses. She was grateful, but he prodded her to look more closely at the flowers. Something was shining up at her.

"A key? What's this?"

"I found a place of my own, I didn't want to say anything until it was official. But I figured you should have a key. I want it to be your home, too."

Her eyes widened and her mouth fell open, but no sound came out of her mouth.

"Is that ok? You don't have to move in. I just mean you can come and go whenever you want," Harry said as quickly as possible.

He wasn't sure if he had made a huge mistake or not. He fidgeted with his own set of keys and looked away from Betty, shaking nervously while waiting for a response from her. Even if she said no, and she didn't want a key, it would be better than silence. The air was heavy, and his heart was pounding out of his chest. Each thump felt exponentially harder than the last.

Betty reached in and pulled the key out of the rose. Running it through her fingers, she closed her eyes, but slowly a grin came across her face.

"This is perfect!" she said.

She jumped up into Harry's arms and whispered in his ear, "We'll have a bed now. We can finish what we started in the cemetery a few weeks ago."

Harry’s eyes lit up and he let out a little laugh as he spun her around.

"Tonight?” he asked.

Harry's apartment was a very bare-bones place to live, but he was happy to have space of his own, and more importantly, a space where he could be alone with Betty. Being alone wasn't always the best thing, though. The summer went by quickly, and Betty was soon swept up in school activities again. She didn’t have as much time for him as he wished she did.

Betty tried her best to juggle things with Harry, her schoolwork, her friends, and her family obligations, but it was tricky. He asked her to come over every night, and as much as she wanted to, it was hard to get anything done around him. Every day seemed to lead to the same fight.

"I have to go to the library tonight. I'll call you tomorrow, ok?”

"You said that yesterday!”

"I’m sorry. I’m getting so close to graduating; I can't mess it up now.”

"Can't you study at the apartment? I'll make it cozy for you!”

"I know you will! That’s the problem! What if I come over for a little while before I head to the library?"

"Perfect!”

For once she wasn’t lying when she said she had to study, but there was something about the look in Harry's eyes that she just couldn't resist.

Things went on like that for the rest of the school year. Betty spent her days in class, her afternoons arguing about whether or not she had time to spend with Harry, and her nights feeling guilty no matter what choice she made. The blissful escape she had once seen in him was gone. Now, he was a chore. She hated to think of him that way. Wasn't love supposed to make all of your insecurities disappear? An unexplainable feeling of failure followed Betty everywhere and pushed her to make sure things worked out with Harry. Maybe love wasn't about enjoying time spent with the other person; maybe it was about spending time with them even when you had almost no interest in it.

Harry's recounting of his workday was always boring and included stories that made it seem as if her father was his best friend. The two would laugh at the same jokes, like two high school kids in the lunchroom, take breaks together, and even sign up for the same overtime shifts! It wasn't that Betty didn't love her father, but one of the things she had found most attractive about Harry was his rebellious side. She was seeing less and less of that every day. Bills were piling up, and he had to be responsible. He had traded his friends for coworkers and was dumbfounded that Betty had trouble walking away from her friends.

"Once you wear that cap and gown, it's over, you know?" Harry said.

"High school? Yeah. I know. That's what happens when you graduate."

"Not just the classes. You'll have no real need to meet those girls for sodas every afternoon, anymore."

"I guess not."

Betty had to admit that he was right. Things would change, and they weren't going to be hanging out at the soda fountain every day anymore. She just hadn't realized how quickly her life would change after crossing out of that stage.

IX.

Ok! To recap, this lady met a so-called bad boy, fucked him in a crypt, and then just wanted to hang out with her friends. She's wilder than I imagined, but still. I'm missing the part where her life isn't perfect. Was it the spider? Did that moment ruin her forever? Olivia thought to herself.

Try as she might, Olivia couldn't help but want to hear the rest of Betty's story. Yes, it was all very perfect, but wasn't everything in the beginning? With a bit of a lull in Betty's storytelling, Olivia started to think about Cole again. Did he expect she would make a drastic change after graduation? What would that even look like?

After that evening at the food truck festival, things seemed to be locked in for Olivia and Cole. He started expecting they would see each other daily, and she was more than ok with that. They would wander around the town, finding little coffee shops to frequent, and establishing a routine of their own.

Their dorms were close enough for them to meet for breakfast, but only if they both committed to waking up early. Olivia had class at 9:30 three days a week, so she was forced to be an earlier riser. Waking up in the morning was a lot more difficult than she had expected. When she was making her schedule before the semester began, she thought she would get all of her classes finished early, and then have the entire day to herself. People tried to warn her that it wasn't going to be as easy as she thought, but she'd assumed she would be the exception. She always excelled at scheduling and getting things done in a timely manner. Getting to class on time shouldn't have been a big deal! Plus, she'd had to get up much earlier to make it to school on time when she was in high school. What was the difference? She learned pretty quickly that the difference was not having her mother to make sure she got up in the morning. It was one of those things she just took for granted but making sure you were up and out on time was far from easy.

Cole was always studying, so meeting for breakfast just gave him another excuse to hit the books. The conversation was limited, and Olivia preferred it that way in the mornings anyway. She loved to sit in silence, enjoying her first cup of coffee and mentally preparing for the day. Although the two of them made it a point to meet every morning, slowly they became more like two random people sitting at the same table. There were morning greetings, and there was a quick kiss before they each grabbed their trays, and then Olivia headed straight for the coffee and cereal bar, while Cole took a more well-rounded approach.

"How can you eat so much in the morning?" Olivia asked, staring at his tray full of eggs, bacon, pancakes, toast, fruit, a bowl of oatmeal, a glass of milk, and an orange juice.

"Breakfast is important," he replied.

"I guess, but that's a lot!"

"And you are loading up on sugary carbs and caffeine, so I don't think you are exactly the authority on healthy eating!"

"Whatever."

Olivia hadn't wanted to fight about breakfast, but it seemed like no matter what she said in the mornings, he was offended. She couldn't figure out how to make him happy. He wasn't miserable all the time, but she didn't have the patience for him in the morning. Any conversation that would push his buttons needed to be avoided, so she added breakfast foods to the list of taboo topics. She already knew to avoid anything of importance, so why not add breakfast food to the list?

They finished their breakfasts in silence and said a fast goodbye as Olivia ran across campus for her first class of the day. She thought it would be nice if, just once, Cole walked with her, but he was too consumed by his reading, and she didn't dare ask him to sacrifice his morning study time for her. They would have time together later on, anyway. There was no reason for him to go out of his way for her. She just assumed everyone was like that. Putting yourself first wasn't a crime. In fact, it was something she wished she were better at doing. It was hard to think that maybe Cole didn't care about her, and their relationship was just a matter of convenience. But that wasn't something she allowed herself to spend much time on because she couldn't be sure that wasn't how she felt about him. Her mind took her back to that night in the alley after the food truck festival, and she decided that she was going to surprise Cole with a box of Lemonheads when they met up later that night.

The day flew by. Both Olivia and Cole were excited about their date later that night. Although things were routine and a little boring, they both depended on the little bit of excitement they got from each other. Love and excitement. That was what everyone wanted. She couldn't be sure that's what they had, but in Olivia's mind, it was a good placeholder. That night, Cole wanted to go bowling, and Olivia was happy to get off campus and do something a little different for a change. Plus, the candy she was going to take to entice Cole seemed to fit the retro theme of the night.

"What size shoe?"

"8."

"Ok. I'll get them. You can look for a ball that's not too heavy for you."

"That was a little sexist! You don't think I can handle a big one?"

Cole laughed, unable to think of a witty comeback right away.

"I didn't think you had too much experience with something too big."

"You said it," Olivia said as she walked off laughing.

It took Cole a minute to realize he had set himself up for that one. Olivia's wit was unparalleled. When he walked up behind her, she was entering their names on the scoresheet.

"What should your name be?"

"Cole?"

"Boring!" she replied as she typed it in.

"I'm not boring! What name are you using?"

"Olivia."

She was always trying to get him out of his comfort zone. A little embarrassment never killed anyone!

The couple bowled for what felt like ages. With only two of them, there was almost no time between frames to sit and talk. Olivia kept shaking the pack of Lemonheads she'd brought with her, hoping Cole would hear it and ask about them. Maybe subtle didn't work on him, because he barely looked in her direction.

When they started their second game, Olivia took the box out of her pocket and slowly put a few pieces of candy in her mouth. This time, Cole noticed. He had to be the only person alive who found it erotic, but there was something about Olivia and those candies that he just couldn't resist.

He walked closer to her, and as she put the box of candies out for him to take, he shook his head and just kept moving closer. Olivia's heart was racing faster. She didn't expect him to say no to the candy, but she definitely didn't expect what came next.

Rather than grabbing the candy, he put his arm around her, pulled her close to him, and kissed her. Pushing her mouth open, he ran his tongue over hers and took the candy from her mouth. He pulled away, and smiled at her, teasingly showing the candy he was holding between his front teeth.

"Want it back?"

She pushed up against him, taking the candy back in the same way he had taken it from her. Looking back on it, that was a silly sort of gross little game they'd created for themselves, but it was so playful and fun. That was why she'd brought the candy in the first place. Dating was supposed to be fun.

They turned their attention back to bowling when the piece of candy was gone, but the smiles and flushed cheeks made it hard to focus.

"Are you ready to get out of here?"

"Didn't we pay for a few more games?"

"It doesn't matter. I'm done bowling," Cole said decisively.

Olivia just shrugged, and let him lead the way.

The two of them left, hand in hand, and headed for their favorite coffee shop downtown. It was much quieter than the bowling alley and offered a little bit of privacy.

They walked into the small corner coffee shop, neither of them concerned with having a drink at that moment. Knowing it was all for show because you can't go to a coffee shop and not order anything, Cole walked up to the counter, ordered their usual drinks, and met her at the table she had found in the dark back corner. Olivia tried to concentrate on the coffee in front of her, but Cole made it next to impossible. She watched as he raised his mug to his lips and blew gently in a feeble attempt to cool his coffee. As he looked over the mug, he caught her eye and flashed a coy smile before reaching out to grab her hand under the table. Olivia blushed as his hand crept from hers to her thigh.

"Sorry!" Cole said as he snapped his hand away.

"What? What happened?"

"I think I'm being a little too forward and physical for sitting in a coffee shop."

Olivia didn't disagree, but she also didn't want him to stop. Something was exciting about being out in the open like that. Plus, they weren't doing anything too risky. He touched her leg; they weren't breaking any laws.

"It's fine," she said, reaching under the table and taking his hand again.

Her breathing quickened, and her heart pounded in her chest as she willed him to touch her again. He found his way back to her leg, and gently stroked her inner thigh while looking intently into her eyes, His cheeks flushed, part of him feeling like he was breaking some sort of rule, and the other part driven by a primal desire.

This only lasted for a few minutes before Olivia pulled away from him, smiling but with her eyes looking down in shame.

"Are you ok?"

"Yeah, sorry. I just got nervous."

"Just breathe," he said, reaching for her again.

This time, he put his hand around her waist. As he became more brazen and didn't care to hide their contact under the table anymore, he slipped under her shirt, gently caressing the curve of her torso, following it up to her breasts, and slowly moving back down again as soon as his fingertips grazed under her bra. A pleasant shiver had shot through her, but Olivia was relieved to see there were still some boundaries she didn't have to tell him existed.

"Do you want to get out of here?"

"I thought you'd never ask," she said.

When they left the coffee shop, there was no pretense about where they were going, or what they were going to do. As they walked down the street, Olivia's mind was racing, and for once, it was all positive. She had no doubts about what they were doing. Things were perfect. He was sweet and gentle, but domineering in a way she had never known could be so attractive.

The problems arose the next morning. Something about a passionate night made Olivia believe Cole would have more interest in spending time with her during the day, and maybe they'd have a normal conversation at breakfast. But they walked into breakfast and fell into their typical routine. He went overboard, she kept it quick, and they acted like they barely knew each other.

Aren't we supposed to be more connected now? Olivia asked herself.

She knew better than to have expectations, so having them about Cole confused her. She started to think she'd let things move too quickly. She hadn't followed a plan with him, and she always followed a plan. Life without a detailed plan was a disaster waiting to happen. The idea of leaving things to chance was foreign to her, but so was quitting. She went on as if it didn't bother her that things weren't magically perfect between them. The sexual chemistry was undeniable, and she seemed to melt any time Cole brushed his fingers against her, even in passing. There was no walking away from that.

Although she told herself to relax and just go with the flow, she couldn't help but think about how things were or weren't with Cole. That didn't stop her from pretending things were going well though. She decided the only option was to follow the trusty adage, "Fake it til you make it," and hope that things with Cole would start to feel as perfect as she had hoped they would.

They would alternate between meeting in her room and his, neither one of them wanting to annoy their innocent roommates with an unwelcome guest too often. That was often Cole's excuse for not spending the night: he didn't want her roommates to hate him. It was only fair that they did not have to share their space with him as well as her. It always made her wonder if he even wanted to spend time with her. What an easy excuse. She didn't want to upset anyone, and certainly not the people she lived with and her boyfriend's friends. That was bound to complicate things, and that was the last thing she needed.

Hi, Jen! Have a minute? she texted her friend.

Yeah. Wanna call me in a few?

Sounds good.

Olivia needed to get some clarity, and Jen could usually help her find that. This time, she was nervous. She had secretly hoped Jen was too busy to talk on the phone so she would have to muddle through things with Cole on her own.

"Hey! What's going on? You ok?" Jen asked when she picked up the phone.

"Yeah. I'm ok. Just feeling a little weird about Cole."

"Always! That's always your problem! What happened this time?"

"Sorry. I'm not trying to annoy you with my relationship bullshit. I'm just bad at this, you know?"

"No. No need to be sorry. I'm not annoyed. I didn't mean to sound insensitive. What's going on?"

"I'm just worried that he doesn't want to spend too much time with me. He's always looking for an excuse that neither one of us can control."

"Like what?"

"Our roommates. He thinks we are putting them in uncomfortable situations when we spend the night with each other."

"Are you that loud?" Jen laughed.

"Shut up! That's not the point!" Olivia said through her laughter.

Laughter provided a much-needed break. It was hard to worry too much when you were laughing with your best friend.

"Seriously though, he says they probably hate us because we are taking up space that's meant for them. They are being affected by a relationship they didn't ask to be part of."

"Hmm. Honestly, it's not totally invalid. Are you guys at least considerate? Invite them to watch a movie with you sometimes or whatever?"

"Of course! I thought we were all friends, but Cole has me thinking everyone actually hates me."

"I doubt that anyone hates you. And if they do, fuck 'em!"

"Always clutch with usable advice, Jen!"

She didn't want to know what Jen would say when she told her she was starting to think Cole had no feelings for her but just liked that she provided him with company and some physical intimacy. Maybe he didn't think she was a very good person. Maybe he thought she was boring, and maybe he hated spending any time with her when it meant they'd have to talk to each other.

Olivia already knew but wouldn't admit it.

You're projecting. Maybe it's you who can't give up the need Cole is meeting for you, not the other way around, she pictured Jen saying to her.

Olivia closed her eyes and tried to shake off the insecurity she was feeling. Maybe it was just an awkward rough patch in their relationship. She decided that everyone had those. And if she was wrong, and this wasn't a normal part of relationships, then she would need to figure out an exit strategy soon.

As the couple entered their sophomore year of college, there was very little change in their relationship, but Olivia was choosing to keep dealing with the insecurity she was feeling. Part of her knew things were supposed to be better, but the other part of her started to believe all of the negative stuff was just in her head. Of course, she hadn't, for even a second, thought that both of those things could be true. Maybe things could be better, and maybe they weren't as bad as her mind was leading her to believe. Her solution was simple enough. She stopped pushing Cole to spend so many nights together and made sure they made the most of the time they had alone. She had friends she could be spending more time with, but as her mother loved to remind her, she was paying tens of thousands of dollars to learn something, not to win a popularity contest or find a husband. Although she usually ignored her mother's advice, this she took to heart. It was time to buckle down and get things accomplished, academically. Of course, this was a little redundant for Olivia, who was always right on top of her schoolwork, but a little extra studying never hurt anyone.

Following her mother's advice, Olivia started spending more time attending her professors' office hours, just to make sure she got a little face time with them, which she believed would help her grades. It wasn't that she went every week, but she made a point to take advantage of the opportunity to talk through big assignments and ask questions before exams. That was when things first seemed to get complicated for her with Dr. Jenkins.

She took her first class with him that year, and she was enthralled by the material. She had always enjoyed learning about how people lived, and her first sociology class was helping her gain an even better grasp of humanity. The syllabus alone had excited her. The topics started with major figures in sociology, research methods, and the foundations of society, and continued to include gender, race, age, and economics. It truly felt like there was a little bit of everything in that course. She was simultaneously excited and overwhelmed.

By midterms, she had been to the professor's office at least five times, and he always seemed to expect her when she knocked. She wasn't sure if he was happy to see her, or annoyed, but she loved talking about the subject matter and picking his brain a little more outside of class, so she continued to go. It seemed to her that the study guide for the midterm was much more involved than any she had received for her other courses, and she needed to get some clarity. Would all of the things on the study guide be on the test, or was this just all of the information they had covered during that half of the semester?

Olivia tried to explain that to Cole when he asked her to get dinner with him instead of studying. This was unusual for him to do, but it seemed like he wanted more and more time with her and she was less willing than ever to give up any of her study time, especially if that included office hours with Dr. Jenkins.

"I don't understand why you need to go again!" he yelled at her.

"I don't give you a hard time about studying instead of paying attention to me!" she yelled back.

"But I'm not going to hide out with a female professor in her office! In fact, I'm right in front of you half the time!"

"I don't see how that's relevant."

"Well then, you must be blind," he said somberly.

It was the biggest fight they had ever had, and Olivia thought about not going to check with Dr. Jenkins about the midterm, but as her mother had said, she was spending all of that money for an education, not a husband. She wiped her tears and headed to the sociology department to meet with the professor as she'd planned.

When she knocked on the office door, she heard an exasperated Dr. Jenkins tell her she could come in. She reached into her pocket before opening the door and found both a small box of Lemonheads and a little container of mints. She looked at both, thought about how upset Cole was with her, and then how important the man behind the door was. She took a mint and opened the door.

"Hello, Professor."

"Ms. Standford, what can I do for you today?"

"I just wanted to talk about the study guide for the midterm. There's a lot of information there. Will all of it actually be on the exam?"

The look in Dr. Jenkins's eye told her that was a foolish question. Of course the things on the study guide were going to appear on the exam. Why would he have wasted his time creating a long and detailed document if it wasn't meant to be used?

"Not everything is a trick, you know. Just study the material. You'll be fine. Do you have any specific questions?"

Olivia wished she had prepared more for the discussion they were having, but she was so caught up in her fight with Cole that any preparation went out the window.

"Umm. Well, I'm a little unclear about the effects people like Piaget and Kohlberg have had on our current study of sociology."

"That's a pretty heavy question. I know you've done the reading. You always participate in class. I can give a quick overview though. Piaget laid the foundation for Kohlberg. They agree about moral development, but Kohlberg takes it a step further. He says that people aren't just considering what is right and wrong on a personal level, but that as your moral development continues, you start to consider how your choices affect society as a whole. How that affects our current study of sociology? Well, it changes how we look at people."

As he was continuing with his monologue that she had all but begged him to perform for her, Olivia was almost awestruck. She was listening to his explanation, but she already knew all of that. At that moment, she was fixated on the confidence he was showing. Someone who so confidently understood so much about humanity must have a much clearer view of emotions. Happiness and despair, pleasure and pain, must be things he could experience for himself and elicit from another person easily.

"And so, to understand society, they help us realize we must first understand the individual," Dr. Jenkins concluded.

"It's so fascinating," Olivia said, placing a mint in her mouth.

Dr. Jenkins ran his hand over his jawline, stroking his beard, making eye contact with Olivia at the same time. She couldn't look away. Cole didn't have a beard, and she started to wonder how it felt. She could almost feel the professor's eyes on her, and her breath caught in her throat for a second when he spoke again.

"You're not going to offer me a mint?"

X.

Betty tapped Olivia on the shoulder and turned a pack of gum in her direction.

"Gum dear?"

"Oh, no. I'm all set. Thanks."

"I thought it would help wake you up. You seemed a little out of it there for a while."

Olivia was slightly annoyed with this sudden need for constant engagement that Betty seemed to have, but she just smiled at her.

"I was just thinking about something. A little lost in thought, I guess. Are you doing all right?"

"Yes. I'm surviving. This is a pretty long flight, though. Don't you think?"

"Definitely a long flight! I wonder where we are."

Olivia reached for the screen in front of her and searched for the map tracking their flight.

"Ah! Just over the ocean. Nothing exciting."

"Jack loved when we were just flying over the ocean. He thought it was the most awe-inspiring thing imaginable. How we could be over the water, with no land in sight, made him giddy!"

Olivia let out a little laugh.

"I never thought about it, but it is pretty amazing. It wasn't that long ago that this would have been impossible. Now we can travel across the world with barely a second thought."

"The world changes faster than we realize. It's like you look up one day, and nothing is the same as it was the day before."

Olivia raised her eyebrows and nodded in agreement.

"That's true."

An air of sadness seemed to sweep over Betty, and she had a very dazed look on her face. With glossed-over eyes and a quivering upper lip, it was obvious to Olivia that she was going to start crying.

"But change is good, right?" Olivia said with a smile, hoping to bring Betty out of her melancholy moment.

There was no need for that. She was talking to Jack again. He always seemed to cheer her up and crush her soul a little bit at the same time.

Nothing's the same, Jack.

No. It's not the same. It's better!

Better? It can't be better when I'm all alone!

You're not alone. We're talking right now. And, you have a young lady next to you, hanging on your every word.

I think I'm boring her.

Impossible! Keep going!

Betty looked over at Olivia and smiled. This girl was so kind to be entertaining an old lady like her. It was obvious she was going through something herself. The story seemed to be distracting her. It was hard to tell if the distraction was wanted, or a major annoyance. She wasn't hearing any objections, so she decided to listen to what Jack had told her to do: keep going.

"I got a little distracted for a minute there!" Betty said.

Olivia looked around for a second, wondering why she even cared to entertain the lady, but she was pretty invested in the story at this point.

"Ummm, you were talking about Harry and high school graduation, I think."

"Ah, yes! I remember. That was a tricky time for the two of us. Transitions usually are. I told you, nothing stays perfect."

Betty drifted back to the conversation they'd had when she was about to graduate. To her, high school graduation signified the end of her childhood. She would be free to do whatever she wanted, without the stress of tests and homework. To Harry, her graduation meant something even bigger.

Harry stood behind her in the mirror, smiling at her as she got ready.

"I'm so proud of you."

She smiled back and continued getting ready without saying a word.

"I'm so lucky to have such a smart woman in my life."

"Yeah. You need someone to balance the checkbook!" Betty said with a teasing look in the mirror.

"I'm bad with numbers, what can I say? But that's not the only reason I want you around."

"No? Why else?"

Harry was silent for a few minutes. He was running through every reason in his head, and nothing he could come up with seemed to be enough. He figured if they had all day, he could stand there and list everything that made him want to keep her, but they didn't have time for that. He wasn't one for being sentimental, and she knew he loved her. Telling her again didn't seem like it was enough. It needed to be bigger than that.

"You've got a nice rack. Don't find ones like those every day," he said.

Betty pretended to be outraged, but she couldn't help but laugh. He may not have had the right words, but he could always lighten a situation. She gave him a devilish smile, shook her chest at him, and asked if he was ready.

"Let's go! The sooner you walk across that stage, the sooner I can take that robe off of you!"

"Is that all you think about?"

"No. I think about watching you pick it up off the floor when we're done, too."

"I have to get dinner with my family after the ceremony. You're just going to have to live this little fantasy out on your own!"

Harry just smiled and reached for his pocket. He ran his fingers across the hard-to-ignore bulge a few times before he realized Betty could see him, and he wasn't ready for that yet.

“We’ll see! Let’s get you to the school. Don’t want to be late.”

The couple joined Betty’s family in her father’s car for the ride down to the school. Her mother’s perfume was so heavy it practically choked them all. But it was a special occasion, so no one dared question her. It wasn’t every day that she had an excuse to wear her expensive perfume. Usually, she smelled of roast chicken and hot rolls. No one ever complained about that, either. There were countless times in her life that Betty wished she could have bottled her mother’s scent. Her graduation day wasn’t one of them.

"Remember to look at us and smile for the picture, honey. We only have one shot at this!”

"I know, Mom. I’ll make sure I find you before my turn so I know where to look.”

"My smart girl!”

"Like a trained monkey, I know where to look for pictures!”

"Ok! That's enough!" her father chimed in.

It didn’t matter anyway, because they had just pulled into the school parking lot. It was time to get started. Betty joined her classmates in the hallway outside of the auditorium, all buzzing with excitement for the future, but also just to be done with high school, which felt like it had lasted forever.

"Listen up, graduates! We will be entering the auditorium in a few moments. Make sure you are in alphabetical order so there are no mix-ups when names are called. Walk quickly, and stay standing in front of your seat until you are told otherwise. There will be a brief greeting, the principal will say a few words, your valedictorian will give his speech, and then you will receive your diplomas. Let's keep things orderly!"

Lining up with her classmates was more chaotic than Betty thought it should have been. But she chalked it up to nerves and excitement. Graduating wasn't something that happened every day. This was a special day for all of them, no matter what their futures held. She tried to keep that in mind and cut her classmates some slack. She was going to miss this little slice of insanity when it was gone!

"Pomp and Circumstance" played over the loudspeaker and the line started to move into the auditorium. Betty was sure to get a glimpse of where her family was sitting so she wouldn't disappoint her mother and ruin any pictures of her walking across the stage. Once all of the formalities were completed, the principal signaled for the graduates to be seated, and he began his speech. Betty was barely listening to him, and she was fairly certain none of her classmates were doing much better.

He introduced the valedictorian, who stood up and gave a run-of-the-mill speech, paying tribute to the teachers and parents, before saying their graduating class was one that would make changes in the world. They would be world leaders and diplomats, teachers, lawyers, and doctors. Betty thought the whole thing was ridiculous. He was supposed to be smarter than the rest of them, and all he could come up with was a list of careers? None of the graduates in that room were going to amount to much, at least if the caliber of that speech was any indication.

Finally, the graduates were invited to stand as the handing-out of diplomas was beginning. Betty smiled at the girl next to her. They had nothing in common aside from names at the end of the alphabet, but it was strangely emotional when they shared an excited glance.

Having a last name that began with a W gave her a lot of time to think and get nervous about crossing the stage. Was she supposed to move her tassel? Did she have to keep a somber expression? Were cartwheels permitted? Betty had no idea why she was suddenly so full of questions. Maybe it was the finality of it all. Maybe it was the crowd. Maybe it was the unknown future. She decided it was a little bit of everything. There was no way a single thing would make her as nervous as she was.

"Miss Janice Waldo..."

Betty patted her neighbor on the shoulder and smiled, encouraging her to start moving across the stage.

"Miss Elizabeth Walker..."

That was Betty's cue. She took a confident stride forward before realizing she needed to slow down for her mother to be able to take a picture. She reached the principal, smiled, and reached out for a handshake with her right hand, and the diploma was received simultaneously in her left. She smiled wider and thanked the principal while trying to pose for her mother, who was several rows back in the crowd. She figured she wasn't going to get a very good picture, but it wasn't Betty's fault. She moved her tassel to the other side and finished walking across the stage and back to her seat. Janice, whose name she had just learned minutes ago, hugged her and the two celebrated quietly at their seats.

After the last few graduates returned to their seats, the principal officially presented the class of 1963, and "Pomp and Circumstance" played once again as they filed out of the auditorium, no longer students, and officially expected to be productive members of society.

When Betty found her family waiting for her outside of the school, Harry grabbed her from behind and swung her around by her waist. She let out a playful scream and pounded gently on his shoulder, pleading with him to let her down.

"I'm so proud of you! Congratulations, Miss High School Graduate!" Harry said as he lowered her to the ground.

"We're all very proud of you! And, more importantly, I think I got a good picture of you too!" her mother added.

"Priorities, Mom. Pictures are more important than anything else!" she laughed.

"You'll thank me for it down the road. Trust me."

"Let's go eat!" her father interrupted.

"Yes. I'm starving!" Betty said.

Harry took her hand and they followed her parents to the car. She was surprised that Harry was so excited for her. However, she also knew he thought this meant she would spend every second with him going forward. That wasn't what she pictured for her future. She needed to find a job and think about setting some goals for herself, but she knew he wasn't going to be the moon her world revolved around.

Her father pulled up in front of their "fancy" restaurant, and Betty wished they hadn't made her keep her graduation gown on. There was no telling when she would ever have an excuse to come back to a place like this again. But she hid her frustration and walked into the restaurant with her head held high, albeit awkwardly adorned with a cardboard graduation cap.

"Congratulations!"

"Well done, young lady!"

"The best is yet to come!"

It seemed like clichés and platitudes were being thrown at her from every direction as they walked to their table. Betty simply smiled and muttered "thank you" as they passed the eager restaurant-goers, none of whom she knew.

When the hostess handed them their menus and walked away, Betty couldn't hold her annoyance in anymore.

"Can I at least take the cap off now?"

"But how will everyone know you're special without it?" her father asked.

"Oh yes. Take it off if that will make you more comfortable," her mother said with a hint of annoyance that made Betty unsure about actually taking it off.

Harry was sitting next to Betty, his eyes not focused on anything nearby. It seemed as if he were lost in thought, far from the issue at hand. Betty glanced over and nudged him gently, trying to bring him back to life. His exuberance had disappeared between the car and the table, and she was confused. He should be happy. It was a nice day, and they were going to eat a delicious meal together. Life was looking good, but his face told another story.

Betty was starting to get worried. She thought maybe it was too much for him to see her take such a big step forward in her life today. They had been doing well when he was the one moving forward in life, but now that it was her turn, maybe things would be different. She hoped things would be different, but that didn't necessarily mean leaving Harry behind.

The waitress came over to take their orders, and Harry perked up. He eagerly ordered a whiskey and soda without giving it a second thought. The rest of the table ordered water, and for a split second, a look of shame passed across his face, until Betty's father ordered the same. Their dinner orders were placed, and they all waited patiently for their drinks to arrive. Once they had, Harry focused on the ice floating in his glass instead of making eye contact with anyone.

Suddenly, he closed his eyes, took a deep breath, and rose from his seat. Betty's father looked at him with a furrowed brow, warning him not to ruin a perfectly nice and incredibly expensive dinner for everyone. Betty's heart was pounding, and thoughts were swirling through her mind faster than she could handle. No one knew what was going on. Harry reached for his drink and took a sip to calm his nerves. He looked at Betty and smiled.

"Son. If you're giving a toast, you're supposed to say something! What is going on here? Sit down," her father said, motioning for Harry to get back in his chair.

"It's not a toast, sir. Sorry. I'm a little nervous."

"Harry? What are you doing? You're scaring me," Betty said quietly.

"Betty. I know that today is a day you have worked hard to get to, and you have achieved so much. I am so proud of you. But I'm proud of you in ways no one else is. I'm proud to introduce you to my friends as my incredibly beautiful, kind, and brilliant girlfriend. I'm proud to get to spend all of my free time with someone so incredible. I'm proud that you choose to spend your time with me. And I'm proud that you make me a better person. You have taught me to love and be loved. You have made my life better in every way imaginable. And I can't go back. I can't be the person I was before you. Together, that's where we strive."

He reached into his pocket and pulled out a ring box.

Ah, that explains the bulge! Betty thought.

As he opened the box, he knelt in front of her before continuing to speak. He thought that was how things were supposed to be done. He hoped so anyway.

"Elizabeth Patricia Walker, I cannot imagine living one single day without you by my side. I love you more than I ever thought I could love anyone or anything. Will you do me the honor of marrying me?"

Her father shook his head in anger and disbelief, muttering under his breath, "I told you not to ruin this dinner!"

A look of genuine shock was plastered on Betty's face. This had been the last thing she expected to happen. Graduating from high school was supposed to have been the most life-altering part of her day. She would have liked it to be the most life-altering part of her summer as well. It seemed like there was about to be more change than she could handle for such a short period of time. When her parents had told her life moved faster than people realize, she didn't think they meant it went by so quickly she wouldn't be able to catch her breath between adventures. A boring summer would have been nice, but a wedding sounded pretty nice, too. A voice crept up in the back of her mind and asked the most important question she could ever choose to ignore: *But do you love him?*

Betty looked around the table at her family. Her father was a shade of red she had never seen before, and her mother was looking down at her place setting, gripping her glass of water so tightly Betty thought she could see it start to crack. She knew no matter how she answered this question, she was going to have someone important to her left feeling disappointed, angry, and hurt. She hated thinking that one word she was about to utter was going to have such a huge impact on the people in her life. There was something she found slightly flattering about that, but her ego aside, she knew she needed to answer the question so poor Harry could get up off of his knee.

She closed her eyes and then took one more look around at the three most important people in her life. Something was about to change, and she hoped she wasn't going to make the wrong choice.

As she inhaled nervously, she took Harry’s hand in hers and smiled.

“Yes!”

“Oh, thank god! You were really making me nervous there.”

Harry lifted her in the air, the same way he had when she had walked out of the auditorium earlier that day.

“Well this day went to shit!” her father declared.

Her mother whispered in his ear, and the look in his eyes softened a little as he nodded in agreement with what she was saying. Betty had no idea what they were talking about, but she did appreciate that her mother’s words had magically calmed things down.

When the waitress came with their food, her father ordered a bottle of champagne, telling her they had a lot of things to celebrate that evening.

"My daughter graduated from high school and got engaged on the same day! How incredible!”

"Congratulations! I will bring that champagne right over, sir.”

"Thank you!”

When the waitress came back with the champagne, Betty’s father stood up and raised his glass. After clearing his throat, he smiled at Betty and nodded.

"Elizabeth, Betty, as you like to be called, you changed my life forever the day you were born. Nothing will ever match the feeling a father has when he sees his daughter for the first time. I was the first man to love you, and I will continue to love you, with or without your permission because that's what fathers do. We love without question."

He paused for a minute and just stared at Betty, who was getting a little teary-eyed. She smiled softly at him as if to say she understood, and she loved him, too. Harry pulled her in closer to him, putting his arm around her, and holding her tightly.

"Happy tears, right?" he whispered.

"Of course. Only happy tears today," she said quietly, without looking away from her father.

He gathered himself enough to continue the speech.

"Betty, you are the most important thing in my life, and I hope I have shown you that you should never settle for second best. You should have high standards and even higher expectations. If you believe Harry can exceed your expectations in life, then you are making an incredibly wise choice."

Betty smiled and tried to ignore the extra level of doubt her father had just planted in her mind.

"Now, Harry. You didn't ask for my blessing, and I thought we were friends, so I'm a little offended. But, lucky for you, she said yes. I'm not sure why, but that's not for me to worry about. You seem to understand that Betty is incredible, way better than someone you deserve, and still, she has chosen you. Love her. Cherish her. Provide for her. And always know that I'll kill a man if he hurts her."

Harry laughed nervously, understanding there was at least a sliver of truth in his last statement.

"To both of you, congratulations!"

He raised his glass a little higher and signaled for the rest of the table to join him.

"To Betty and Harry on this momentous occasion."

The family clinked their glasses together before sipping their champagne. Life was about to change for all of them, and there was no way to slow it down. Betty sipped her champagne with a taut smile and all the nerves in the world. She hadn't expected the day to go the way it had, and she wasn't sure she'd made the right decision. She kept asking herself if she was truly in love, or if it was just a rebellious phase she was going through. She was anything but pious and pure when she was with Harry. Was that what made her feel so attached to him? The rule-breaking adrenaline rush he always took her on?

"Want to come to my place tonight? Have a private celebration?" Harry whispered.

Betty looked at him and nodded slowly. This was their future. Private celebrations for big moments would be the most exciting part of their lives together.

When they finished their dinner and arrived back home, her father took her by the arm and pulled her in to hug her.

"Betty, I meant it, I do love you, and I will kill him if he hurts you. Just remember, you can always change your mind. This is just an engagement. People cancel them all the time."

"Dad! That's really what you want to say to me the day I get engaged? This has been a really big day for me, and you are trying to get me to change my mind?"

"I'm letting you know I support you, and you have options."

"You're right. The option I'm choosing tonight is staying at Harry's!" And she stormed out of the house.

Harry was waiting for her, and pulled her tightly into an embrace, kissing her passionately, before they started walking towards his apartment. Holding Harry's hand and walking down dark and largely empty streets, Betty thought that it was the best walk she had ever, and would ever, take in her life. Her first walk with her fiancé, her first walk as a high school graduate, and her officially walking away from her parents' control. It was liberating! She was making a life for herself, and there was nothing anyone could do to change that.

When they reached the apartment, Harry offered her a beer to kick off their celebration. She took a few sips but had other ideas for how the night was going to go, and she knew Harry wouldn't mind. In fact, she was fairly confident that they were on the same page.

"I think being engaged made you better at that!" she said, kissing his neck.

"I was going to say the same thing to you."

"It's probably true!" She laughed.

Part of her believed that this sudden sense of freedom made her less reserved and more eager to experience things. Granted it wasn't exactly a new thing for her to do with Harry, but her inhibitions were less than they had been.

Harry kissed her again but then pulled himself away from her.

"I have to work in the morning. Your dad is already going to be pissed off. I can’t add being late to the list of things he hates me for,” he said.

"He’s all bark! Get back here!”

"We have plenty of time,” he assured her.

They laughed together, but Harry was right, there was no reason to risk being late for work. There would be other nights like that in their future.

The couple had decided on a shorter engagement than Betty’s family would have liked, but when they started to talk about it, there didn't seem to be much of a point to waiting. There would be no extravagant ceremony, no expensive dress, nor would there be throngs of people waiting to watch them commit themselves to a lifetime of wedded bliss.

"What about your family? Are you going to invite them?” Betty asked while they were coming up with their guest list.

"No. What’s the point? My mom will be hammered, and I don’t even know where my dad is. Useless. I don’t want to waste a stamp on them.”

“But you could call? That wouldn’t be wasting a stamp. I worry that you’ll regret not asking them to be there for you. It’s your family.”

"You're my family now. I barely needed them growing up, and I definitely don't need them now. End of story!"

"Ok. Smaller is better anyway."

Betty had never really asked about his family. She knew he had moved to this apartment hastily after he started working with her dad. She just thought he was sick of being pestered by his mom all the time like most teenagers were. Slowly, she started to figure out that things were much different growing up in his house than they were in hers. Of course, Betty found her parents overbearing, and there was something very scary about her father at times. He had even convinced a few of her friends that he was a mob boss, so they were petrified of him for a while. But he was harmless. Typically, he was grumpy after a long day at a job that he was always a little too secretive about, but that wasn't the worst fate Betty could suffer. Some kids complained all their dads did was talk about work. It was kind of fun for his job to be a mystery to Betty when she was younger.

Harry, on the other hand, was surrounded by trouble. His dad was pretty secretive about his work as well. But it was possible that he actually worked for the Mafia. He dressed well but didn't have an office job, and he could end a bar fight with a single icy glare. And while Betty's mom was at home making dinner and cleaning, Harry's mom was the reason for the bar fights his dad had to end. She was a bit on the wild side and didn't seem to have a maternal bone in her body.

His life had been hard, and he always spent his nights dreaming about having a perfect family like Betty's. When he'd seen the opportunity to be part of a family by getting close to Betty, he was overjoyed.

The prospect of building his own was something he couldn't wait on. He was confident that his life was coming together the way he had always hoped it would. He had found love and stability. He had a good job, and a nice apartment to call his own. There was little he could complain about.

Harry wasn't too worried about the wedding plans. He figured Betty would make sure things went smoothly, and he would just make sure he showed up. It wasn't that simple though. Betty wanted to plan together. It was about both of them, after all.

"My mom said there's no way she's letting us, or more accurately my dad, pay for a caterer when she can just make the food for us. So, I guess that's what we'll do. Now we just need a cake."

"Ok. Sounds good to me. Nothing too fancy, nothing too big. Other than that, it doesn't matter."

"Right. We can go down to Carmello's tomorrow and put in our order. I can't believe how fast this is happening!"

"Not fast enough, if you ask me!"

"You don't like planning with me?"

"I love everything with you! I just can't wait to make it all official, you know?"

"It feels pretty official to me already!"

"It's not. You still live with your parents, and there's no document verifying our commitment. And then the whole 'having our commitment blessed by a priest' thing."

"Fine! Almost official! Two more weeks. I think we can make it."

It seemed like they were having the same conversation on a nightly basis for the weeks leading up to their wedding. They were both a little nervous but entirely overcome with excitement that they could hardly contain. So, it was no surprise that the night before their wedding, Betty found herself in her bedroom, crying with her mother.

"What if this is the biggest mistake of my life? Am I really old enough to be going through with this?"

"Betty, I have all the faith in the world that you are ready. And even if this doesn't end up being the picture-perfect marriage that I'm sure it will be, you're smart and capable. It will all be ok."

"Ok. I do love him, you know?"

"I know. That's why it will be perfect. You love each other, and that's the most important thing."

"Were you nervous before you got married?"

"Nervous? Oh, Betty, I was ready to hop on a train and run away!"

The next afternoon, when the couple arrived at the church, it was nearly empty. A few pews were filled with Betty's friends from high school, one with her aunts, uncles, and cousins, another with her grandparents, and, naturally, the first was reserved for her parents. On the other side of the aisle, Harry had managed to get a couple of his friends to put on shirts and ties, but there were no family members. When Betty looked out before the ceremony began, her nerves were different from the night before. She was no longer nervous about committing to Harry; she was nervous for him. Quickly, she asked her mother to see if a few people from what was perceived as her side would move over to even out the pews. She would have been heartbroken if so few people had shown up in support of her, even if that was what she'd expected.

Her mother ran down in a hurry and whispered to a few of the girls, who took their dates by the hand and shuffled across to help fill in the other side of the church. Whatever Betty wanted on her wedding day was going to happen. As the music started and she walked down the aisle, arm in arm with her father, she knew she was ready to take this step. If she could think of him first, everything was going to be just fine. She knew, had the situation been reversed, he would have done the same. When her father handed her over to Harry, he leaned down and quietly whispered, "Thank you," in Betty's ear. Whether he was expressing gratitude for having her friends mix with his, or simply for marrying him, she never knew for sure.

The rest of the ceremony went off without a hitch. They walked into the banquet hall and were announced as Mr. and Mrs. Harold Fredricks. It seemed like as soon as they arrived at their table, Harry's friends were eager to buy everyone drinks. Round after round of whiskey, gin, and vodka, with beers peppered throughout, was brought over to Harry, and he could never refuse. Clinking glasses rang loud over the music, beckoning the newlyweds to kiss, over and over again. And each kiss from Harry was a little sloppier than the last. The alcohol was so strong on his breath that Betty started to believe she was going to get drunk just from kissing him.

"Maybe no more drinks?" she whispered.

"Married for all of two hours and you already think you can tell me how much I can drink!"

"I'm not telling you anything. I'm just wondering what you think."

"I think I like drinking."

"I can see that! But it is our wedding night, and that might affect other... things. You know."

"My things will be just fine! Calm down. Why don't you drink with me?"

She let out a ragged sigh but grabbed the glass sitting in front of him and finished his drink. She figured she might as well enjoy the reception as much as her husband was. The idea that he was her husband made her giggle. It felt so right but incredibly weird to say he was her husband. Not her boyfriend or fiancé, her husband.

When it was time to cut the cake, Harry and Betty walked over to the cake as they were supposed to. Things were going fine until they needed to slice the cake to feed it to one another. As he was handed the knife, it was clear he wasn't going to be able to do it on his own. Betty grabbed his hand to try to help guide him and spare him the embarrassment of being unable to cut a piece of cake, but he pulled his arm away from her.

"Leave me alone! I can do it myself!"

"Fine. I was just trying to help. You seem a little unsteady."

"Unsteady? Really? If I were unsteady, could I do this?" he asked as he flipped the knife up in the air and readied himself to catch it.

The knife landed nowhere near him and instead fell to the ground next to Betty.

"Thank you for proving my point," she said with her head falling to her hands.

Her mother came running up to the table with another serving knife, and they tried to salvage the moment. Harry submitted and let Betty help him cut the slice of cake, and the two fed it to each other as peacefully as they could. There was no need for more theatrics that would have come from smashing the cake into their faces. People were already trying to stifle their laughter and judgment. There was no need to add to it.

The knife-throwing incident hadn't gone over well with anyone, especially Betty's father, who had already been against the wedding. Any time Harry moved, his eyes followed him. There was no way he was going to let him do any other over-the-top antics to ruin his daughter's wedding day. It was bad enough that he'd persuaded her to commit to a life of mediocrity with him. She deserved one good night, one beautiful memory. He was not letting Harry leave without letting him know what he thought of the show he'd put on for everyone that day, but he also didn't think he would remember anything he heard tonight, so he resorted to yelling what amounted to nonsense in his direction as his friends were escorting him out of the banquet hall.

He had been so drunk that his friends had to help him home that night. Harry, passed out drunk on the couch, would be the truth behind their wedding night. There was no consummation of their marriage, yet. Betty was frustrated that he hadn't listened to her when she suggested he slow down and make sure they would be able to have the wedding night they had dreamed of, but she was exhausted anyway.

Betty got up early, the way she thought a dutiful wife should, and made her husband a big hearty breakfast. She brewed a nice pot of coffee, whipped up some pancakes, fried some bacon and eggs, and slathered butter over two slices of toast. She had assumed that would be enough to rouse Harry from his drunken slumber, but he took a little more convincing. She curled up next to him on the couch and ran her fingers through his hair, whispering for him to wake up for breakfast. His eyes opened as if they were weighted down, and he shut them again, stretching while he nodded at her.

That was all he needed. He dragged himself to the kitchen, sat down, and eagerly took a sip of coffee.

"I'm sorry."

"I know."

The two ate their breakfast in silence after that. Maybe this was marriage. A big fight could be fixed with hot coffee and a simple apology. Betty started to believe they were going to be just fine.

"I need to talk to your dad."

"He's livid. You need to go to him with more than a quick apology."

"I'll figure it out. Would a bottle of whiskey be appropriate?"

"If you want him to throw it at you, sure!"

Betty never knew how Harry made amends with her father, but things cooled down pretty quickly. A few months into their marriage, Betty was pregnant, and the focus had changed. Harry was working as many overtime shifts as he could in hopes of being able to afford all of the baby's needs. The idea of being parents when they still felt like kids themselves was a little overwhelming.

While Harry threw himself into work, Betty worked on trying to make their apartment more of a home. She wanted everything to be clean and safe, and when people came to visit the baby, because people always wanted to visit babies, they wouldn't think that she was an unfit parent. She hoped her friends would come over, hold the baby, and think it was incredible that they had built such an amazing life in such a short time.

For Harry, the time seemed to fly by. He was barely with Betty while she was pregnant. It wasn't that he was avoiding her, it was that he was afraid he was going to be a poor provider, and he was going to make sure that wasn't true. It was the opposite for Betty. Yes, she was trying to build a better home for the baby, but she was lonely, and there was only so much she could do to fix the apartment up when she was by herself.

XI.

"And in November, we welcomed our first baby boy, Joe," she told Olivia.

"Wow! You must have been so happy!" she said.

"Happy, scared, overwhelmed, exhausted, and I wouldn't have changed it for the world!"

"But you did get your happy ending with Harry. I don't understand why you were telling me that your life wasn't perfect. It still sounds that way to me!"

"I'm not even close to done yet. I need a little break, though. Can you push the button for the girl to come back again?"

"Yes. Of course."

Olivia pushed the call button, wondering why she couldn't have done that herself, but decided there was no reason to have mean thoughts about this sweet old lady. As Betty grew silent, Olivia found herself slipping right back to her own memories. She was back in Dr. Jenkins's office with him asking slyly for one of her mints.

"Oh, you want one?" she said, caught off guard.

"Only if you're going to give me one."

She thought she had to be imagining things. There was no way the professor was being as flirtatious as she thought. Maybe he sincerely wanted a mint. While she dug the tin of mints out, she couldn't help but think of Cole, and his far-fetched concern about her spending so much time with Dr. Jenkins. Cole being right about that would kill her.

He can never know about this! she thought.

She held out the tin of mints for him to take from, and he shocked her. He did reach into the tin and take a mint. But he also grabbed her wrist, not letting her back away as he placed the mint, slowly, on his tongue. Although she was being held, motionless, nothing was forcing the prolonged eye contact she maintained with him. The intensity of the moment swept her away.

“This is a lovely mint, Ms. Standford,” he said.

Olivia tried not to laugh at him. She thought that was the strangest thing to say, not only in that particular moment but ever. What classifies a mint as lovely?

“I’m glad you like it, Professor.”

“Do you ever think about how mints make your mouth feel? Is it a sensation you think is describable?”

“I think you can describe anything. How well you capture something is another question.”

“Ah! That’s why I like you, Ms. Standford. Smart and funny.”

Olivia’s mind played that over and over again. This professor, the one she wanted so badly to impress, thought she is smart and funny? How was that possible?

“Thank you,” she said in a shaky voice.

“But not so confident, I notice!”

Olivia looked down at her feet, trying to hide her embarrassment.

"Don't look away from me," he snapped.

"Sorry," she said instinctually.

He still hadn't let go of her wrist, but he loosened his grasp a little, moving his hand up her arm. He traced from where he was holding her wrist, up her forearm, along the inside of her upper arm, and to her shoulder. She was frozen. She didn't dare move away from him, but she wasn't sure she wanted him to continue. She also wasn't sure she wanted him to stop.

When he reached her shoulder, he continued across to her collarbone. She shuddered, and her heart was pounding. Not only was she in a committed, although imperfect, relationship with Cole, but this man was also an academic advisor and professor. There were so many things that she knew were wrong with the situation.

"Professor..."

Silence.

"Professor! What are you doing?"

"I think you know. There's no use denying what we both know we want."

Olivia was worried that he was right. She did think about a moment like this more often than she would ever let him know. She couldn't want that, though. This wasn't the sort of thing that was part of her life plan. She never pictured herself being unfaithful to a boyfriend, and she couldn't even imagine herself having an affair with a professor.

But he was so attractive. And there was something about the attention he was giving her that went beyond what Cole could provide her. His approval of her on an intellectual level brought her a kind of satisfaction that she didn't think could be found anywhere else.

While she was busy trying to decide if she wanted to put a stop to this encounter or not, he was busy making sure it continued. He moved in closer to her and whisked her hair behind her ear, blowing softly into it, before gently nibbling her earlobe. She was starting to feel more powerless than she had before.

Before she could attempt to pull away from him, he moved in to kiss her. Olivia did not back away, and kissed him back, finding herself mirroring his every movement. She had never felt so in sync with someone she was kissing before. She started to wonder if it was some sort of sign about how things were or should be with Cole. Or maybe, what she did with Dr. Jenkins had nothing to do with Cole. She preferred to think that they were completely separate, but she knew they weren't. There was something bad, something rebellious about being physical with her professor. Something that was erotic in a way Lemonheads could never match.

Without a word, Olivia and Dr. Jenkins had moved behind his desk. He sat her on the desk, and stood in front of her, positioned between her legs. This was something Olivia had thought only happened in movies, but there she was. Her arms were strung around his neck and he continued to kiss her, with his hands resting on her thighs. She knew what was happening, and the battle between guilt and pleasure was in high gear. No matter what happened next, even if she walked away right then, she was sure she would never be able to look Cole in the eyes again.

She moved her arms from around his neck and intertwined her fingers with his. When he backed away from her, she noticed that the sides of his lips curled in an unfamiliar way. It was a smile Olivia had never seen out of him before. He wasn't exuding happiness, but rather accomplishment. He had exactly what he had wanted. Olivia's heart was pounding. There was anticipation for the pleasure she was sure awaited her, but the presence of fear and regret was overpowering that.

There had been very few times in her life that Olivia felt the way she did, sitting curled around her professor. Of course, how was someone supposed to feel in a moment like that? As a person who tended to be hyper-focused on what she was supposed to be doing, and what was right versus what was wrong, it was not a situation she had ever imagined for herself. To Olivia, there was an order to things. Like everything else in her life, she had a list for that as well.

- ❑ Friendship
- ❑ Attraction
- ❑ Building a relationship/dating
- ❑ Love
- ❑ Sex
- ❑ Marriage
- ❑ House

- ❑ Children

Not on the list? Affair with a married professor, who did not check many of the boxes himself. With him, she felt something different, something so enticing it bordered on sinister. The idea that you could have admiration and lust in place of friendship and love had never crossed her mind.

The added risk of going so far from the plan scared her. Would an illicit affair be her undoing? What if someone found out? Would she be kicked out of school? She found herself in a thought spinout that was all too familiar. Every choice she made started one of these tornados in her mind. She had once explained to a friend that she was a lot like Dorothy, swept up in a tornado she should have been more prepared for. But for her, there were no munchkins, talking scarecrows, lions, or tin men teaming up with her to fight against a wicked witch. It was her, alone, with her thoughts.

Sometimes, even the strongest storm couldn't sweep you away. There was something about the feeling she had with Dr. Jenkins that kept her present. Yes, she was thinking about how sleeping with him wasn't part of her plan, and it was beyond destructive for everyone involved, but with him, standing so close, his breath hot on her neck, her conscience would need to pull a little harder for her to walk away.

"I don't know how this is going to help me on the test."

"It'll help you relax. Relieve some stress! I can see it in your shoulders. Let go!"

"But the test."

He moved back to kissing her lips, partially because he couldn't resist, but mostly because he needed her to shut up.

"I have to do well on the test!"

"Oh trust me, you'll be fine," he said as he grabbed her waist and lifted her off of the desk.

Olivia gave in. She knew fighting the magnetic pull that was between them would never work. Flushed and breathless, she forgot about the test for a minute. If she could have stayed in that moment, wrapped up with the professor, she never would have made her way back to reality. The familiar buzz of a cell phone jolted them both back to reality. They shared a sense of panic looking for their phones to see who needed to come back to reality a little faster than the other. It was Dr. Jenkins's phone, but it snapped them both back to reality.

"Ok, I'll stop for milk on the way home. Anything else? Sounds good. Love you too."

He had errands to run for his family, and Olivia was reminded that he had one. She hurried and got dressed again while he was on the phone, hoping to just sneak out the first chance she had. But he noticed her and put a finger up, signaling for her to wait a minute. He hung up with his wife and pulled Olivia back in for a long hug and an invitation she wasn't sure she could refuse, but she knew she shouldn't accept.

"I'll let you know. Thanks for the help, Professor." And she walked out of his office, overwhelmed, satisfied, nervous, and at peace. Each feeling inside of her was at war with another feeling. Before she could handle any of it, she had to decide what she was going to tell Cole. Was this a one-time thing that she could keep a secret from him? Breaking things off now might raise suspicions. And did she even really love him? He never made her feel the things she'd just felt in Dr. Jenkins's office. But her mind soon went back to her list. Cole checked the boxes the professor never could. Would it be in her best interest to walk away from this person who was exactly like what she pictured finding for herself as a life partner? The idea of being the "other woman" in someone's marriage felt dirty. But in some ways, dirty was enticing; dirty only strengthened the pull on the professor.

Walking across campus, Olivia was trying to stay focused on the trees. Fall in New England was always so beautiful, and she loved to walk down the tree-lined pathways. The vibrant colors, the crinkling noise beneath her feet, and the crisp chill of the autumn air were usually enough. They could transport her from whatever stressful situation she found herself in, and allow her to be present in the moment. There was no getting past what she had just done. You couldn't simply get over something like that, especially given the person she had done it with. Not to mention, whom she had betrayed. Could you love someone and betray them?

A warm, familiar smile greeted her when she got back to the dorms. Cole pulled her into a tight embrace, and she crumbled in his arms.

"Oh my god! Are you ok? Liv, what's wrong?" he said, holding her tighter to make sure she stayed on her feet.

She couldn't stop the tears. Still having no idea what, if anything, she was going to tell him, she knew she needed to be right there, in his arms. Something about having him squeeze her close, let her feel his heartbeat against her own, made her feel safe in a way that surpassed any other sense of security in her life.

XII.

Taken back to that afternoon, in a messy and poorly lit dorm room, Olivia realized that was the sort of thing Betty must be holding on to. That was the kind of memory that made you want to talk to someone. But still, she wasn't sure. She glanced over at Betty, who had closed her eyes for a minute. She looked so peaceful. This serene nothingness was on her lips. The thought passed Olivia's mind that she was very old. Maybe she should check to make sure she was still breathing. She was a little too still for her peace of mind.

Slowly, Olivia reached out a finger and gingerly poked Betty in the arm, jabbing so gently at first, she wasn't sure she had touched her. There was no reaction.

Oh great! The old bitty Betty died on me! she thought to herself, not sure what to do next. It didn't take her too long to decide she was overreacting. She was probably a deep sleeper. She just needed to get up the nerve to try again. This time, Olivia used three fingers to tap quickly on Betty's shoulder.

"Betty?" she said. "Are you ok?"

No answer still. She wished she was the type of girl who wore makeup because they always seemed to have mirrors, and if she had a mirror she could try to see Betty's breath like they did in those old detective movies her grandfather had always made her watch with him.

"Hey! Betty! Are you alive?" she said louder than she had intended as she grabbed her shoulder and shook her.

There was nothing at first, but then the woman started to move. She stretched, opened her eyes, and smiled at Olivia.

"What's wrong? Was I snoring?"

Olivia laughed. "No. I was afraid... Well, I was just lonely. I really want to hear more of your story!"

"Patience is a virtue, my dear."

"I'm sorry to have woken you. I was just hoping to get out of my own story for a minute."

"It must be quite a doozy if you're running all the way across the ocean to avoid it."

Olivia just looked down, fighting back the tears that had started to well up behind her eyes. This perfect stranger had her completely figured out. She realized that running away from her problems was a stereotypical thing to do, but she hadn't been sure of any other options. She needed to have space. Space from her family. Space from her classes. Space from Cole. And space from Dr. Jenkins. There was no figuring her life out when the influence from all of them loomed large. She didn't want to disappoint anyone, and she didn't want to make the wrong, and possibly immoral, choice.

"Would you like me to pick up my story? That should help distract you. You don't even know the half of it yet!"

"Please! Your perfect life is such an inspiration!"

Perfect life. Those words echoed in Betty's mind. Her heart started to beat a little faster as she felt the pressure Olivia was putting on her to have lived a life worth hearing about. Her eyes closed tightly for a minute.

What do I do, Jack? Should I keep going?

Oh, Betty. You have to keep going. You know you do. There's so much happiness left to share with her.

Hearing Jack in her mind, she knew it was her only option. She had to keep telling the story. This was her shot to tell it without having to be worried about the fallout. Taking a sip of her now lukewarm coffee, Betty steadied herself and tried to pick up the story where she had left off.

"I told you about having baby Joe. He was such a good baby. Thinking about it takes me right back to those days," Betty said, with a misty look in her eyes.

Right back in those first few months with Joe, Betty knew her life was changing, and those would be the moments she would remember for the rest of her life. Holding a fragile life in her arms felt a lot heavier than the six pounds and eight ounces he'd weighed in at birth. Holding him was simultaneously the most calming, natural thing, and one of the scariest, most paralyzingly important things she would ever do. She worried about dropping him or crushing his little toes when she put him in pajamas.

She had thought it was scary when she held that tiny life in her hands. She had no idea it would be even more frightening to have Harry hold him. Sure, Joe was his son, too, but he was so rough. She worried he would hold him too tightly, or even worse, shake him! It didn't take more than a week of sleepless nights for her to let Harry take care of him on his own when he offered. Harry, it turned out, was an incredible father. She hated to admit it, but he was better at swaddling him than she was.

Harry's face would light up when he got home from work and went over to swoop Joe up from his crib, even when Betty objected, saying she had just gotten him to fall asleep.

"You're with him all day! Let me have some time with my son!" he would say as he lifted Joe out of his crib and spun around in a circle.

"He's going to throw up on you, and you'll deserve it!" she snapped at him.

"You do the laundry. I don't care if my clothes get dirty!" he said with a laugh.

Betty shook her head, knowing it was true. Housework was never-ending, it seemed. It used to be something she relished doing well. After Joe, she just wanted to get it done so she could sit down for a minute before he needed something else from her. All of the crying and dirty diapers were enough to make her swear off sex for life, out of fear she would have more babies and more messes!

She loved the moments she had when Joe cuddled close to her and made little cooing and gurgling noises. Those always melted her heart a little. They always brought a smile to her face, and she would try to engage him in a made-up conversation.

"Oh yeah? I know!" she said softly to Joe.

"A-aaa!"

"Wow! What a story!"

She would try to keep him looking at her and making those little noises for as long as she could each day. She had no idea, but she thought maybe it would be good for him to hear people talking to him. Harry would talk to him, too. Betty loved when she got to listen to him give little pep talks to their crying son or try to reason with him when he just wouldn't go to sleep.

"Come on, little man! I've got to get up early for work in the morning, and if you let me sleep now, I'll make sure you get the best bib money can buy!"

Joe seemed to be mocking him as he just made more noise. In time, it seemed as if Harry realized there was no reasoning with him, and talking to him in the middle of the night wasn't going to make things any easier. He just needed to rock him. Betty always felt like she was missing out on something when Harry was rocking him to sleep in the living room. All she could do was stare at the bare white walls and listen to the back-and-forth motion of the chair. The sound of the chair's rhythmic motion would make her eyelids heavy, and she always drifted off to sleep before Harry returned to bed.

Harry may have stayed up making sure the baby got a good night's sleep, but it was Betty who pried herself out of bed before the sun. Her to-do list was long, and she had no choice but to start early. Harry needed coffee as soon as he woke up, followed by fried eggs with a side of bacon every morning. Plus, she needed to be ready for Joe. He would need clean diapers and breakfast. Before she could do that for Joe, she had to make sure Harry's lunch was prepared and packed for the day. If it wasn't ready for him to grab and go, she knew there would be no calming his temper. A morning fight with Harry was predictable and all too common. It felt like every day it was the same thing all over again.

"Ham again? Can't you change it up once in a while?"

"Yeah, sure. I'll get right on that and make you a gourmet lunch tomorrow. I have all the time in the world with a crying infant demanding all of my attention!"

"God, you're so dramatic. Just forget I said anything."

It almost didn't matter what she made Harry for lunch, because she knew he would complain. Like clockwork, as soon as Harry gave her a quick, emotionless kiss and a gruff goodbye, Joe cried. And day after day, she held Joe and cried with him. She wasn't sure she was made for the life she was living. Betty missed her friends and having someplace to be without a baby in tow.

The longer she spent at home, tending to Joe and serving Harry, the less she cared about anything. Every day was robotic and mindless. It just wasn't the life she had pictured for herself. It wasn't until her mother stopped by for an unexpected visit that anyone mentioned the change in her.

"Betty! What is going on over here?" her mother asked with a tone of genuine concern.

"Nothing. I'm just taking care of Joe," she said, shrugging.

Her mother shook her head.

"This isn't like you. There's laundry everywhere, unwashed dishes in the sink, and pans on the stove! It's a disaster in here."

"Thank you for pointing that out. I'm sorry I'm a little busy taking care of my newborn son and his helpless father!"

Betty's eyes filled with tears as her mother furrowed her brow and pulled her in for a hug.

"I didn't mean to criticize. I'm just worried."

Through her tears, Betty let everything out.

"I'm so sad all the time, and I know I should be happy. I have a husband who is working hard and providing a decent-enough life for us. And more importantly, I have this beautiful, perfect little baby boy but I still feel empty. I have so much guilt because I miss my friends, and I would give just about anything to go out and spend time with them, just pretending I didn't have a baby to worry about. There's so much I want to do that I can't do with a baby. Maybe I made a huge mistake."

"You're just tired, dear. It'll get easier. You have to try harder for this little one. He needs a stable home with a mother who smiles at him all the time and tells him how much she loves him. Don't be cold."

And just like that, her mother's attention was focused entirely on doting on her new grandson. Joe was her first grandchild after all, so who could blame her? His chubby baby cheeks were crying out to be pinched, and Grandma had lots of kisses to give.

Smiles at him all the time? Betty thought to herself. That didn't strike her as the most important thing for a healthy childhood, but it was better than yelling all the time. She knew her mother meant well, but that didn't make it any easier to just smile and be happy. There wasn't a magic switch she could flip to make all of her feelings positive.

Time. It takes time, Betty repeated over and over again in her mind. She only hoped if she said it enough, she would start to believe it.

XIII.

An unfamiliar, but not altogether foreign, cry caught Betty's attention.

"Babies never stop crying, huh?" Olivia quipped, obviously annoyed with the infant on board the plane.

"It seems that way!" Betty said.

"That's how you felt with Joe?"

"Between his tears and mine, I was drowning."

Olivia just gave her a half smile, not quite sure what to say to that. The way Betty explained it, it was as if she'd gone from being overjoyed at the birth of her son to fully regretting having him.

I haven't even gotten to the terrible stuff yet, and she's already judging me. I knew I shouldn't have told her my story, Jack!

Nonsense. She needs to hear this. You're doing fine. I'm right here with you, Betts.

I don't know.

Take a breather. Let her talk for a bit.

"I don't know how you were able to take care of a baby when you were my age. I know I couldn't do it. I don't even like to babysit for too long!"

Betty smiled and sighed. It was as if Olivia had felt the discomfort and hesitation Betty was having while telling her about life with a newborn baby.

"Oh, it's nothing like babysitting when they're your own."

Olivia nodded, pretending she knew exactly how different it would be to have a baby of her own. It didn't stop her from wondering, though. She had never talked about babies with Cole before, but of course, why would she? They were basically kids in their own right, and college was no time to think about babies. But she wasn't really thinking about babies with Cole. She couldn't let go of the conversation she'd had with him after her unexpected encounter with Dr. Jenkins.

Cole's dorm room was a safe haven for her, even when things weren't perfect. So it was only natural that she ran there and into his arms when she was overwhelmed with guilt and uncertainty. When she had finally collected herself enough to pull away from him, she had a story to tell.

"Are you ok?"

"Yeah. I'm just really stressed about this exam, and that meeting with Dr. Jenkins didn't help me feel any better about it."

"He didn't give you any direction?"

Olivia scrunched her nose and tilted her head a little.

"He did direct me. I didn't really take much of it in I guess."

"I'm sure you got more out of it than you realize."

Olivia couldn't believe she was lucky enough to have Cole believe in her the way he did. Sure, he wasn't an acclaimed scholar or anything, but his opinion mattered to her.

"I hope you're right. If I don't get at least a B, my GPA won't be good enough for a decent grad school."

Cole's eyes widened.

"Grad school? That's new. For what?"

"It wasn't really in my plan to go right away. I need to work, but Dr. Jenkins convinced me in class the other day."

"Ok... what did he say that got you thinking like that?"

"A bachelor's degree is basically a high school diploma these days."

"Bullshit!"

Olivia just shrugged. She didn't believe her undergrad would amount to nothing, but she was nervous. Her thought tornado had been amped up when the professor made that comment during class. And she couldn't help but feel like his opinion was important.

"Yeah, I know," Olivia said with a sigh.

"Plus, your GPA is fine! What is it now, 3.6?"

"3.75, actually!" she said, cracking a smile.

The two broke out into laughter. Olivia knew she would be fine no matter what. The pressure she felt was a phenomenon of her own making. And she had to worry even more about Professor Jenkins. Would he be upset that she had stopped their encounter? Would that affect her grade? She hoped he had more dignity than that, but she wasn't too sure. But her mind went back to the last question he had asked her before she left his office. She hadn't given him an answer because she hadn't even been able to process the words. As she was laughing with Cole, and realizing that she was going to be fine, although perhaps not as perfect as she had hoped, Professor Jenkins's words came flooding back to her.

"Let me make you dinner. Come over. We'll have wine and talk about the exam."

Why would she want to go to his house? It wasn't going to lead to anything good! She was also worried that if she said no, he would start to dislike her. She didn't want to risk that, but she also didn't like pushing the barriers. As she thought about it, looking at Cole, she revisited her checklist, but this time she was focused on life with Cole. How many boxes did he check?

- ❑ Friendship? Definitely!
- ❑ Attraction? No question!
- ❑ Building a relationship/dating? Yeah, that was exactly right.
- ❑ Love? Maybe. That was a little trickier.
- ❑ Sex? Oh yeah!
- ❑ Marriage? Maybe some day.
- ❑ House? Not there yet.
- ❑ Children? That was a big step!

Cole was checking four boxes without a doubt, and the others seemed like they wouldn't be far behind. Professor Jenkins, on the other hand, wasn't on the same track.

He checked off different boxes in her life. Sure, there was attraction, but it was more like admiration, infatuation, self-loathing, doubt. Olivia wasn't sure if she was meant to be with Cole, although it looked that way on paper, she knew she wasn't destined to be with Professor Jenkins. Still, she wasn't sure what to do about the invitation.

"So, while I was in the office Professor Jenkins invited me to his place for dinner and wine and studying."

"Sketchy!" Cole quipped. "Are you going?"

"I didn't give him an answer. But I feel like I have to go!"

"Why? He can't make you spend time with him."

"I know, but he can have a pretty significant impact on my future."

"It's your call. I don't think you should go, though."

Olivia just nodded quietly. Her eyes darted around the room as if searching the cluttered dorm for all the answers to life's biggest problems. As the two sat silently for a few minutes, Olivia searched the annals of her mind for an answer to what seemed like an unsolvable problem.

"Hey! I have an idea!"

"It's about time. I could see the steam coming out of your ears, Einstein. What's the big revelation?" Cole asked with a laugh.

"You're such a jerk! What if you come with me to his house?"

Cole closed his eyes and shook his head.

"Your solution is to bring an uninvited guest along with you?"

"Well, he's married so I would assume his wife will be there. It's only fair that I have backup!"

Of course, Olivia hadn't told Cole the whole story of her office-hours encounters with the professor, but there was no way that would come up in conversation if she weren't alone with him. To her, the plan was perfect. She wouldn't be rejecting the invitation, and she would be showing the professor that she was already committed to someone else. Maybe that would make him back off without feeling rejected?

"Ugh. OK. I'll go with you, but I'm telling you, this is not a great plan. I think he's going to be pissed that you invited someone to his house."

"I'll deal with it," Olivia said with a shrug.

"When is this supposed to happen?"

"This weekend, I think."

Cole shrugged and nodded half-heartedly.

Olivia wrapped her arms around him, feeling safe, knowing he was there for her, even when he didn't have anything to gain. She could not wrap her mind around the idea that she had found a man so willing to be there for her, and was not convinced he was absolutely "the one." Truth be told, she wasn't sure if she believed in soulmates or destiny. But Cole was getting her to rethink her aversion to the idea.

"Will you do me a favor?" Cole asked.

"Sure, what's up?"

"Don't obsess about this for the next few days. I know how you get with those thoughts spinning in your mind."

"My thought tornados. I know. I can promise that I'll try."

"All right. That's all I ask," he replied as he leaned in to kiss her gently.

Olivia knew she wasn't going to stop from worrying or obsessing, but if she wanted Cole to be on board with her plan, she knew she had to keep all of that to herself and mask it as best she could. Luckily, she was an expert at hiding her feelings. Her family wasn't exactly big on sharing their emotions. What was typically a pitfall for her came in handy this time.

Back in her own dorm room, she knew she had to respond to the invitation. Rather than risking another one-on-one visit to his office, Olivia sat down to send Professor Jenkins an email. Usually, an email was a quick, thoughtless thing for her, but this one felt heavy. Her nerves were on edge as she stared at her laptop, wondering how her words would be interpreted. Should she avoid anything that could send the wrong message? Should she act as if nothing had happened? Should she tell him she enjoyed the thrill? Should, should, should! Olivia was always concerned with what she *should* do, so how did she get into this position in the first place? Slamming her laptop shut, Olivia grabbed her bag and headed out. Coffee, fresh air, and space always helped, so she headed for the secluded little coffee shop that she and Cole frequented.

It hadn't taken long for the barista to become familiar with the couple, and Olivia loved it! She had always imagined being a "regular" somewhere.

"Hi Liv! Here alone today?" the bubbly barista, Pippa, asked.

"Hey, Pip. Yeah, I need some space."

"Well, this is the perfect spot for that. You're only like the third person to come in all day."

"Nice! Darkness, quiet, and the smell of coffee are exactly what I need today."

Pippa just smiled and nodded her head. "What can I get for you?"

"Ummm. Just a large black coffee. Nothing fancy today."

"Sure thing. Give me a minute to brew a fresh pot for you."

"Thanks."

Olivia's eyes darted around the empty coffee shop. The dark wood paneling was reminiscent of an old saloon in a classic Western movie she had watched with her grandfather while growing up. When her eyes focused on the corner where she had first sat with Cole, the memory of that night flooded back to her. Her insecurity, her hesitance, his hesitance, and their mutual desire. Was that better than what had happened with Professor Jenkins? It was, without question, more ethical. She started to recognize that the night with Cole and the meeting with Professor Jenkins both felt slightly wrong but hard to walk away from.

"So, where's Cole today?" Pippa asked, handing Olivia the coffee she had ordered.

"In his room. I needed a little bit of space to think things through."

"Things? Are you guys ok? Not to put too much pressure on you, but the two of you are my personal Ross and Rachel."

"Ha! Umm... Yeah. I'm just trying to figure some stuff out," Olivia said with a shrug.

Pippa nodded and a little smile crept over her face.

"I'm sure you'll figure it out."

Olivia bit her lip, let out a deep breath, and forced a smile.

"Thanks, Pip."

Olivia looked around the empty coffee shop, wondering if she should stay there, or go back to Cole. But she knew before she saw Cole again, she had to get her head on straight. There were important decisions to be made. Taking a deep breath, she scrolled through her email inbox and started to compose a new message. Should she start, *Dear Professor Jenkins*, or should she keep it casual and use his first name? Didn't Google hold all the answers? For a second, she contemplated googling, *What to call your professor after you make out with him in his office*, but she knew there wouldn't be any good answers there. They would likely all be about sexual harassment, and Olivia didn't see herself as a victim. She was smarter than the girls that were taken advantage of. Wasn't she? Was it bad if she kind of liked it? Olivia tilted her head back, closed her eyes, and let out a deep sigh before returning her attention to the blinking cursor on the empty e-mail message.

One more deep breath, and she began to type:

Hey...

I've thought about your invitation. I accept. 7:30 on Friday?

- Liv

She took another deep breath, closed her eyes, and hit send. What was the worst that could happen? Cole would be there, so there was no way the professor would be anything but professional, right?

"Need a refill?" Pippa asked when she walked past Olivia's table, trying to stay busy wiping down the already clean tables.

Olivia glanced down at the half sip of lukewarm coffee sitting in her mug and nodded.

"Coming right up!" Pippa turned on her heels and walked back behind the counter.

"Thanks, Pip!" Olivia shouted to her. "Sorry, I'm so preoccupied today."

"No worries! I'm here to work, not be entertained."

Pippa walked back to the table, placing the steaming mug in front of Olivia.

"Anything else I can get you?"

"No, I'm good."

As Pippa walked away, Olivia called after her.

"Any chance you have time to talk?"

"Well, I don't know. It's awfully busy in here today!"

The girls laughed as Pippa took a seat at the table. Olivia was stuck in one of her self-proclaimed thought tornadoes, and some perspective was needed to help her pull out of it.

"I did something dumb, Pip! Really, really dumb!"

"Doubtful, but what happened?"

Olivia raised her eyebrows and shook her head.

"You're not going to believe this. You know Professor Jenkins, right? I think I remember you telling me about a class you took with him last semester."

"The silver fox? Oh, yes. I know all about him. He was having an affair with his TA. Well, that was the rumor anyway."

"Seriously? How do I miss out on all of the gossip?"

Pippa laughed. "It's just my job. People tell me their deepest secrets, and I give them coffee."

Olivia shook her head, not believing it was that simple. Although it was the least of her worries at that moment, she couldn't help but feel like it was personal. She was unwanted, a social outcast, a loser. Then again, maybe Pippa thrived on gossip in ways she hadn't realized. Telling her what had happened with Professor Jenkins might not be the best approach for Olivia.

"That makes sense. You know everyone, so you're bound to get all the gossip."

"Well, I think the Silver Fox's affair is just public knowledge at this point though. Why did you bring him up?"

Olivia shrugged, still unsure if she wanted to tell Pippa everything that had happened and the situation she found herself in.

"He's my advisor, plus I have a class with him this semester, so I've been in his office a lot recently. I didn't see an issue with it before, but Cole has been really bothered by the amount of time I spend with the professor."

Pippa squinted her eyes and tilted her head. "Ok? That's a little weird."

"Right? I don't know why he has been so against me spending time with a professor, trying to make sure I do well in his class."

"Is that what you guys are fighting about?"

"Ehh, we're not really fighting about it. I'm just struggling. I was invited to dinner at the professor's house, and Cole doesn't think it's a good idea. I think it's important that I go."

Pippa's eyes widened and eyebrows rose.

"I know. It's weird! I get that," Olivia said in a defensive tone.

"Hey, I'm not taking sides. It's your call."

"We're not fighting about that, though. I just don't know what I should do. I mean, I accepted the invitation, and am taking Cole along with me, but I don't know if that's right either."

Pippa just nodded.

"No thoughts?" Olivia asked, feeling like Pippa was judging her for not handling things better. It was easy for Olivia to know that she should do well in school and she should prepare for her future. But it wasn't so easy to figure out exactly what she should do in this situation. It was never part of her life plan to get involved in a complicated relationship with a professor. She was barely prepared for a fairly easy traditional relationship like she had with Cole.

"I can't tell you what to do. It's just dinner though, right? So, why not. Making connections is important professionally, so it makes sense to me that you'd go."

"Exactly! I tried to say that to Cole, but I never know what I should do."

"Should, should, should! That's just going to drive you crazy. Do what you want. I'll tell you what my grandmother told me when I was freaking out and called home freshman year: Don't 'should' yourself."

Olivia smiled and laughed a little to herself. How had no one told her that before? She had always been so concerned with what she should do. That was how she believed she'd gotten to where she had in life. Maybe it was getting in her way?

"Thanks, Pip. Your grandmother sounds cute."

"Oh, cute, sassy, tough. She's everything I strive to be as an old lady who doesn't care what anyone thinks."

"I think you're already halfway there. You just need to get old," Olivia said with a laugh.

"Well, thanks!"

"Think I can get a refill?"

"It is my job, but how about some decaf? I think you're worked up enough and caffeine is just going to make it worse."

"Ugh! You really are an old lady! You're the coffee boss; I'll drink what you give me."

Pippa nodded and skipped off to the counter to make Olivia's coffee.

Olivia opened her email to see if there was anything from Professor Jenkins. Her leg bounced nervously up and down under the table as she waited for her email to load. The Wi-Fi was painfully slow for a coffee shop so close to a college campus. When her email finally loaded, a bold black headline caught her attention.

Jenkins, Charles: Re: Dinner invite

She let out a slow deep breath as she moved the cursor slowly toward the e-mail. Her thought tornado was ramping up.

XIV.

"Oh! The wind is strong, don't you think?" Betty asked, pulling the sleeves of her cardigan down over her hands.

Olivia scrunched her nose, not knowing what wind Betty could possibly mean. They were on a plane, so if there was wind they were all in trouble. Olivia let out a little laugh, realizing what Betty meant. She reached up and closed the air conditioner that was blowing right on Betty's face.

"I didn't even notice how high that was! It was blowing you away. Is that better?"

"Yes, dear. Thank you. I never had to worry about those things when I was traveling with Jack. He just knew how to make me comfortable all the time."

Betty's eyes looked glossed over, and her chin quivered a little before she cleared her throat and jumped back into her storytelling with Olivia.

"It's funny that in my old age, I'm cold all the time. It makes me long for the summer heat of my apartment with Harry. That first summer was a challenge. Not only did I have my first child to take care of, but there was also a heat wave like you wouldn't believe."

To leave the windows open or closed was a big debate for Betty and Harry.

"We have to let the air circulate! Open the windows. We can't have our baby living in this stale, sweltering air," Betty argued.

"That's the dumbest thing I've ever heard. Why would we want to let more hot air in? God, Betty! I thought I married someone smart."

Betty shook her head and rocked the baby back and forth. There was no arguing with him. She knew, of course, that she was right. It was absolutely ridiculous to think that they would never open the windows. With beads of sweat glistening on her forehead, she swiped the back of her hand across her face and wiped the moisture onto the leg of her shorts.

"Oooh, I know! Daddy is being so mean to us!" she said, making sure Harry heard her.

Harry just rolled his eyes and walked towards the door.

"I'll be home later than usual tonight. One of the guys is leaving, so we are all going out for a few drinks after work."

"Money for beer, but no money for a measly fan to keep your wife and child comfortable? I see how it is."

Harry walked out the door without another word. Betty knew he'd be in no shape to continue the conversation later either. The frustration was palpable. It seemed that even baby Joe knew better than to give his mom a hard time that day. His little red cheeks, wet with sweat, broke Betty's heart. She had always hated the hot and humid New England summer, but being powerless to rescue her baby from his first heat wave made it worse.

Betty laid a blanket on the living room floor and put Joe down.

"Your daddy might not think it's a good idea to have the windows open, but what he doesn't know won't hurt him," Betty said in a singsong voice as she went around the apartment, unlocking and opening all of the windows. At the very least, it would provide a breeze. The stagnant sticky air in the old apartment was suffocating.

Her nightgown, drenched in sweat, stuck painfully to her body. No matter how she pulled at it, it seemed to stick more. Uncomfortable cries came from the living room, and she knew she had to find a way to cool them both down. She certainly wasn't going to sit around in the nude with her child all day.

"If your daddy weren't so cheap, we'd have a fan to cool us off, Joe."

Wiping the sweat from her brow, she remembered that to bring down a fever, a lukewarm bath never failed. Maybe the same idea would help in the heat.

"I think it's tubby time little man!" she cooed at Joe.

His damp hair was stuck to his forehead, his cheeks red and his skin clammy. Betty knew at the very least the bath would provide a little relief for him. After scooping Joe up off the floor, she carted him into the bathroom, her bare feet sticking to the linoleum floor. The heat seemed to make everything sticky and uncomfortable. The *tutttk* sound echoed her every move. She leaned over the edge of the porcelain bathtub, shaking her head at the grimy ring she just couldn't manage to scrub away no matter how hard she tried. She turned the knob and watched as pale yellow water flowed out of the rusted nozzle. Reaching her hand out, she lost herself in the refreshing coolness of the water flowing over her wiggling fingers like a babbling brook over worn rocks. Looking down at Joe in her arms, she ran her wet fingers through sweat-drenched hair.

"Does that feel better? It's nice to cool off, huh? You want to take a bath with Mommy?" Betty said softly as she prepared herself and her baby for the bath.

Delicately, Betty lifted one leg and stepped into the bath, trying to hold Joe tight to her so there would be no chance of him falling into the water.

"Oooh! That's a little chilly!"

Betty laughed a little at herself, and Joe immediately started with his baby babbling and reached for the water.

"You think it's funny that I'm cold? You're your daddy's son, that's for sure."

Joe just continued to splash and chatter away in Betty's arms. That cold water had rinsed away the discomfort and frustration that had been weighing her down all morning. The relief provided by the cold water allowed Betty to restart her day. She slipped out of the tub, wrapped a towel around herself, holding Joe close to her chest, and walked to her bedroom to prepare for the day. There was no use staying in the apartment and being uncomfortable, so she decided it was a good day to take Joe out on a little adventure.

"Should we go meet some friends? Yeah, we should!" Betty said as she tickled Joe's protruding belly.

After sliding her lightest tank top on and wiggling into her shorts, Betty turned her attention to a now-sleeping Joe. Babies were like dead weight when they were sleeping. It was a blessing and a curse, at least that was what Betty considered it to be. She had to move more gingerly than usual as she tried to maneuver his pudgy little legs into tiny shorts and lift his arms to pull a shirt over his head. One quick up-and-down glance, and she decided there was no need to force his feet into shoes; he wasn't walking anywhere anyway.

"Ugh! Stupid stroller!" Betty muttered as she tried to get it ready for Joe. It had been handed down to her from a friend of her mother, or something like that. She wasn't sure who had owned it before her, but it was rusty, and the wheels wobbled a little bit. Being on the budget they had to live by, free was about all she and Harry could afford.

This isn't how my life was supposed to go, Betty thought to herself. *Diapers, broken strollers, no friends, no career!* Tears started streaming down her face. She had always imagined more for her life.

"Oh, Joe! I love you, but you really ruined my plans, baby boy. It's not supposed to be like this," she whispered as she carefully placed him in the stroller, hoping not to wake him up. When Joe was sleeping, Betty thought she should feel some relief, but that wasn't the case. Any second that wasn't spent worried about Joe was spent mourning the loss of a life she had pictured for herself when she was younger.

She was supposed to be in college. That was what her parents had always wanted her to do, and she worked hard in school. She was more than capable of achieving a higher education than her parents had. She hadn't dreamt of being a doctor or a lawyer, but she certainly hadn't planned on motherhood so soon. In Betty's perfect world, she was off at school, learning new things and preparing for her life as a newspaper editor, or maybe even a journalist. She'd always excelled at grammar in school, and when she found a mistake in someone's writing, it was hard to look past it.

Betty wiped the tears from her face, took a deep breath, and looked down at Joe.

"Ready? Let's go get some fresh air!" she said in the happiest tone she could muster at the moment.

Pushing the baby carriage through the entryway of the apartment, there was a sense of freedom. Suddenly, the air wasn't stuffy and still. A gentle, albeit hot, breeze blew through her hair and Betty let out a sigh of relief. The cool bath had helped but being out of the tiny apartment was even more cathartic than she could have imagined. There was a little fighting with the stroller to get over the cracks in the sidewalk, but a little extra oomph and the walk could continue as if nothing stood in the way.

"Betty? Is that you?" a vaguely familiar voice yelled from across the street.

Betty craned her neck and squinted her eyes, trying to place the voice. She was wracking her brain, but she just couldn't come up with a name. A wave of panic rushed over her as the figure started to jog across the street. Somehow, she managed to plaster a smile on her face as she was pulled into an embrace.

"Oh, Betty! You have no poker face. You've forgotten all about me, haven't you?"

She let out a little laugh. "No. I'm sorry! I was hoping to figure it out so I didn't need to ask your name."

"Don't give it a second thought. We weren't exactly friends, just met in passing, but you're hard to forget."

"And I guess you are!" Betty said with a nervous laugh.

"Touché! I'm Jack. We met once, well sort of met, at the soda fountain a year or two ago."

It was as if a light bulb went off in Betty's mind. They had met before, but Harry had showed up and dragged her off to their secret hideaway in the cemetery. Her cheeks flushed thinking of that afternoon. It was no wonder she had forgotten that she'd met Jack. Much bigger things had happened that day.

"AH! Jack! I remember now. Between pregnancy brain, sleepless nights with a crying infant, and this horrendous heat I don't remember much these days," Betty explained.

"Pregnancy? This little one is yours?" Jack said with a hint of disbelief in his voice.

"This is my baby boy, Joe."

"He's adorable. I just can't believe you're a mom. You don't look like you had a baby."

"No? How do women who've had babies look?" Betty asked with a serious tone of disdain in her voice.

"Umm. Well... I guess I mean you look really good."

"Thanks. You're sweet. I don't remember the last time my husband said that to me."

Jack just shook his head.

"Can I buy you a soda?" Jack asked.

XV.

"Beverages?" the flight attendant asked as she walked down the center aisle of the plane.

"I'll have a soda, please," Betty said.

"Sure thing. What kind?"

"Any kind," she replied with a shrug.

The flight attendant looked over at Olivia, who met her confusion with an equally amused face and shook her head.

"Cola?" the woman asked, unsure of what to give Betty.

"Yes, dear. That's perfect," she assured her.

As she passed the soda to Betty, Olivia asked for a black coffee. The flight attendant nodded. "I'll be back with the coffee."

"Thanks," Olivia said.

"More coffee? Wow! I'm surprised you're not vibrating!" Betty said with a laugh.

Olivia bit her bottom lip. She knew she drank more coffee than most, but she didn't realize how much she'd had on the plane. But was it really her fault that the flight attendant was the most present and efficient she'd ever seen? If someone offered, Olivia rarely declined.

"Wait a minute! You just said Jack! I was starting to believe he wasn't part of your story."

Betty smiled and nodded slowly. Her eyes lit up at hearing his name.

"I told you to be patient. You'll realize that people join your story at all different points," Betty said with a knowing wink.

Olivia couldn't help but shake her head and smile and replay Betty's words over again in her mind.

When the flight attendant returned with her coffee, the rich aroma of a steaming cup of coffee brought Olivia right back to the coffee shop and her stressful e-mail exchange with Professor Jenkins.

That bolded e-mail subject line, **Jenkins, Charles: Re: Dinner Invite**, was screaming for her attention, while also begging her not to open it. Her thoughts were spinning out of control. *Will he be angry? What if he decides I'm too much of a child to interact with anymore? Did I ruin his plans? Will this change how he sees me? How DOES he see me? What if this e-mail is explicit? Would that be such a bad thing? YES! Ugh, I'm the worst! I bet he's mad at me. Oh, god. I really messed up! Maybe I can leave it unopened and pretend he never sent it. No! He's too smart for that.*

Closing her eyes, Olivia let out a deep sigh. She knew she had to read the e-mail. There was no getting out of it now. She'd chosen to take him up on his offer. Now she needed to follow through. She lifted her coffee to her lips, hoping to find any reason to delay opening the email. "One sip before it gets cold," she whispered to herself. The taste of fresh coffee was one of her greatest pleasures in life. Having coffee was an experience for her. The warmth flowing down her throat was relaxing and had a strangely calming effect on her. The taste of perfectly roasted coffee beans brewed exceptionally well at just the right temperature gave her something else to focus on for a minute when she needed to calm the storm in her mind.

She looked back to her computer and slowly moved the cursor over to the e-mail she was dreading. She closed her eyes and clicked.

Sounds good, Ms. Standford. I look forward to meeting the boy who keeps you busy when you're not with me. My wife is making chicken — I hope you're not vegan!

- C

Olivia scrunched her forehead and squinted her eyes. *That's it? Seriously?* she thought to herself. She had been worried for no reason. That e-mail was painless. Maybe she didn't have anything to worry about, and it was all in her head. But then again, what if he wanted things to be tricky because he enjoyed sneaking around? It had been Professor Jenkins's idea for her to have dinner at his house, with his family. Olivia was relieved and confused.

"Are you ok over there?" Pippa asked.

Olivia pursed her lips and thought for a second. Maybe Pippa was the right person to talk to. She may know a lot of gossip, but that didn't necessarily mean she couldn't be trusted to keep a secret.

"Yeah, I'm all right. Just a little confused about some stuff going on in my life right now," she said softly.

"Want to talk about it? I'm pretty good with existential crises."

Olivia laughed and shook her head. "Existential crises? I don't know that I'm having one of those right now. Just poor life choices, maybe."

"Doubtful! But I'm here to listen if you feel like talking," Pippa said.

Olivia bit her bottom lip, contemplating the judgment she assumed she would face if she let Pippa in on what was going through her mind and, more importantly, what had happened with Professor Jenkins. As if on cue, her leg started to bounce up and down and her nerves took over.

"I told you switching to decaf was the way to go. You're so jittery. Slow down with the caffeine, girl," Pippa said as she walked up behind Olivia.

"I don't think it's the coffee. I have a lot on my mind."

"Fair enough. Anxiety's a bitch."

Olivia laughed. "Truer words have never been said."

There was something about the little smile that came across Pippa's face. She didn't have a big goofy grin but she also didn't look like she was just trying to appease Olivia because she was a customer. She couldn't pinpoint it, but something about the way Pippa smiled at her made Olivia feel safe. Her shoulders relaxed as she let out one slow, deep breath.

"Any chance this place will get busy soon?"

"Today? I can't imagine that happening."

"Ok. I just don't want anyone else to hear about my situation. Can you promise this conversation will never go beyond me and you?" Olivia's tone was serious, verging on stern.

"Of course. Think of me as your untrained therapist, and this coffee shop as my office," Pippa assured her.

"Please don't judge me too harshly, ok. I know this is going to sound bad." Olivia's leg was bouncing faster, and her voice shook.

Pippa just nodded in agreement, not saying a word.

Olivia looked up at the ceiling, taking note of the shape of every crack and knot in the wooden beam over her head.

"So, the 'Silver Fox,' Professor Jenkins, and I had an interesting meeting during his office hours," Olivia said with her eyebrows raised, trying to hint that the meeting hadn't been a standard academic meeting.

"Ok," Pippa nodded, encouraging Olivia to keep going.

"Things just felt different right away. He was flustered, I assume because of the girl before me running out in a tizzy. And I didn't even know if I wanted to stay at first. But you know, there's a big test coming up, and I need to do well in this class if I have any hope of getting into a decent grad program." Olivia was barely taking a breath between words.

"Slow down! I'm going to need you to back up to the other girl running out of his office," Pippa said, her once soft and happy face now stern and demanding.

"I went to knock on his door, but I heard some arguing going on. I couldn't hear what they were arguing about, but I figured it wasn't my business. I thought about leaving and going back later, but I was already there, and I needed to talk about the test, so I was determined. Right as I was backing away, the girl came storming through the door and was gone."

"Do you think he did something to her? I mean, that's super sus," Pippa said.

Olivia's thoughts started to swirl. *Oh, she's definitely going to judge me! Why am I telling her this? Maybe I should make up another problem to tell her about and pretend this didn't happen.* She shook her head to try to quiet the thoughts. She had already taken the first step. She needed to keep going.

"I-I-I'm not sure. I don't think so. I assumed they were just arguing about a grade or something."

"Ok, yeah, sorry. My mind goes to assault a little quicker these days. As women, we can never be too cautious."

Olivia nodded quickly, trying to assure Pippa that they were on the same page. She absolutely believed in everything that the #MeToo movement was about, and without question, she agreed that people should believe in women. But this wasn't one of those cases. There was no way anything had happened with the girl before her. That was what she told herself, anyway. She could never know for certain.

"I think we all do that these days. It was my first thought as well, but when she came out, she seemed more focused on the paper she was carrying. Anyway, when I went into his office it started off like a normal office-hours meeting. He asked what questions I had, he got annoyed with my need for specificity and told me as much."

"Right, so what's the real issue here?" Pippa asked.

Olivia brought her hand up to her face, rubbed her eyes, and pinched the bridge of her nose.

"Well, you know he's pretty attractive, and before I knew it, he had me sitting on his desk making out with him."

Pippa's eyes widened and she clasped a hand over her mouth.

"But that's not all." Olivia shrugged as she wondered if she really should tell Pippa what the issue became.

"What? I have no words now, and there's more?" Pippa rubbed her forehead.

Olivia let out a quick breath before starting to explain the rest of her encounter with Professor Jenkins.

"It's not bad! I swear, it's all consensual, and I wasn't pressured." Olivia went silent for a minute. "I mean, he didn't want me to leave when I planned to, but that's just because we were having a good time."

"Did you sleep with him?"

Olivia shook her head emphatically, "No! I mean, we were getting a little beyond just kissing but then his wife called and it freaked me out."

"A little beyond kissing? What does that mean?"

"You want me to lay it out in ridiculous baseball terms?"

"Sure! Whatever you're comfortable with."

"I wasn't serious about that, but I guess second base, rounding to third? Is that a thing?"

"You're a regular play-by-play announcer!"

Olivia shook her head and rolled her eyes at Pippa.

"I knew you'd judge me."

Pippa tilted her head to the side and softened her expression a little.

"No, I'm sorry. I'm not judging you. You can make out with, even fuck, anyone you want. I was just caught off guard. I've always heard the rumors about how much of a creep he can be and I didn't want that to have happened to you."

"I get it. Weirdly, it happened. I swear it wasn't planned."

"It isn't really my business, but does Cole know?" Pippa asked quietly.

"That's why it's even more complicated than it might seem on the surface. Before I could leave his office, Professor Jenkins invited me to his house for dinner."

"Woah! Did you turn him down?"

"I accepted after I talked to Cole. I left out the part about our meeting being anything but academic. And I got him to come with me."

“Wait, what? You’re bringing your boyfriend to have dinner with the professor you cheated on him with?”

“My life is a regular soap opera, huh? But I thought, if he gets to have his wife there, I was having a backup, too.”

“Good point! Why is he having you over at his house with his wife? That’s just looking for trouble if you ask me.”

“I think there’s a sense of excitement, sneaking around right under their noses.”

“Oh, you’re bad! Ok.”

Pippa laughed and Olivia couldn’t help but join her. There was something about sharing that with someone that made her feel a little lighter. The storm in her mind had slowed and she could hear herself think clearly again.

“I don’t think I’m going to tell Cole. Not yet at least.”

“Remember, you are my Ross and Rachel! Don’t break my heart.”

“Ross had a kid with someone else. Rachel was engaged! They are not the perfect couple you’re making them out to be.”

Pippa shook her head.

Olivia smiled at her and started to pack her things. As she zipped her laptop case closed, she added, “Cole is kinda nerdy like Ross, isn’t he?”

“Cute-nerdy, though!” Pippa retorted with a laugh.

"Very true. Thanks for listening to me. Remember, keep that between us. Please."

Pippa nodded and ran her finger over her chest "Cross my heart."

Olivia smiled at Pippa and turned towards the exit. She had to head back to Cole and let him know about their now-official dinner plans. She wasn't hopeful for a cheery response, but at least Cole would be easier to talk to than Professor Jenkins.

"Hey!" Pippa yelled after her. "Keep me posted on the dinner."

Olivia nodded. "Will do."

XVI.

Olivia began to shift in her seat and let out an aggravated sigh before she caught Betty's eye and smiled.

"It's a long flight, huh? I need to get up and stretch a little bit. Mind if I squeeze past you?" Olivia asked.

"Oh of course you can. I should probably stand up, too. The doctor has warned me about the combination of the cabin pressure and sitting still for too long affecting my health. But I don't tend to listen too well. In one ear and out the other as they say."

Olivia nodded and tried to get past Betty as smoothly as possible. Betty was barely standing, so Olivia had to try to step over her without making a fool of herself and falling into the aisle. That alone counted as a stretch in Olivia's mind. She thought about stretching right there in the middle aisle but decided against possibly making a scene. She wasn't convinced that she wouldn't accidentally whack someone in the head while she was moving around. And she could barely stand the idea of a conflict erupting because of her clumsiness. Each of those fears got her thoughts spinning a little, so her safest bet was to stretch in the privacy of the bathroom. Folding her hands behind her back and stretching her biceps, rolling her head in circles, and completing a few quick side bends proved difficult in a cramped airplane bathroom, but Olivia made the best of her situation. Not wanting to stay in the bathroom for too long, she ventured back to her seat.

"All refreshed?" Betty asked as Olivia climbed over her.

"Much better, thanks."

The two women sat in silence, listening to the chatter around them reduce to a murmur as overhead lights were being dimmed and books were being packed away in the seatback pockets. Olivia opened her mouth to speak, but Betty beat her to it.

"I feel like someone's mother just announced bedtime," Betty joked.

Olivia's laugh was louder than she had expected, which just sent both women into a laughing fit. Passengers all around them started to mutter their disapproval and annoyance with the sudden laughter filling the airplane cabin. With a few ragged deep breaths, they were able to quiet down.

"So, where was I? Oh, right! Running into Jack!" Betty said.

"Yes! I need to know more."

Betty drifted back to that hot summer day and a chance encounter on the street.

"Did you really just ask a married woman out?" Betty questioned Jack.

Kicking at the loose gravel in front of him, Jack stammered.

"Umm, well, no. I wouldn't say that." He shrugged.

"In front of my son, no less!" Betty retorted, gesturing to Joe in the carriage.

"No! I swear! It's not like that."

Betty couldn't contain herself any longer. Laughter took over.

"I'm just kidding," Betty said through her laughter. "I'd love to get a soda with you."

She glimpsed down at Joe, who was peaceful for the first time all day. Staying in the carriage for a while longer would be good for him.

"Phew! You scared me there for a minute."

Betty shrugged and bit her bottom lip, proud of how convincing she had been.

"Let's go!" Betty quipped, putting her hand out in front of her and signaling for Jack to lead the way.

Jack quickly slipped in front of Betty and headed straight for the door of Ligget's Soda Fountain. He held the door open for Betty, who had been taking her time following behind him with Joe. It was fun to see a man try to make her happy because the times Harry had really put in the effort with her seemed to disappear after the birth of Joe.

"Wanna sit at the counter, or...?" Jack asked with a shrug.

Betty knew she didn't want to be too close to the windows because she didn't want to risk being seen. The nation may have been moving towards a more liberated understanding of love and pleasure, but she didn't need any rumors to be started about her. Plus, she had a baby to think about.

"It's a little hard to sit up there with a baby. Is a booth in the back, ok?"

"Oh yeah, I'm a dunce! Of course you don't want to sit at the counter with a baby. I'm not so used to being out with women who have a baby in tow."

Betty raised her eyebrows and offered a perfunctory smile as they headed to the booth she had suggested. She decided right there that spending the afternoon with him was a mistake. She would stay and have exactly one soda with Jack and then explain that she needed to take Joe home. She took a seat in the booth and positioned the baby carriage against the wall next to her and waited for Jack to return with the sodas.

"Here you go," Jack said, handing Betty a bottle of TaB.

Betty squinted, took the soda with a grimace, and sat silently for a moment.

"I was going to ask if they were out of Coca-Cola, but I see that's what you got for yourself. Why'd you get a TaB for me?"

Jack shifted in his seat and looked towards the booth next to them before answering her.

"Well, I know women need to watch their weight, especially after they've just had a baby. I figured that's what you'd want."

"Ok. I need to lose the baby weight, huh?"

Betty's cheeks turned a deep shade of red. Why had this man asked her to have a soda with him? Just to humiliate her? Of course he had; there was no other reasonable explanation for the encounter.

Jack shook his head emphatically.

"NO! I'm sorry. I wasn't trying to imply anything. You look fantastic, if I can be so bold. I'll trade drinks with you if you want."

"That's ok," Betty said, looking down at Joe.

The two sat in silence for what felt like an eternity to Betty.

First, he'd insulted her weight, and then he'd stopped talking altogether. It was not how she'd expected the afternoon to go.

If I wanted to be miserable, I could have stayed in the sweltering apartment and waited for Harry to get home, she thought to herself.

Her self-deprecating thoughts were taking over, and that confident woman walking down the street, who had agreed to spend time with this man, was gone. She slowly sipped her soda, trying to hide her disgust for the diet drink. She knew the ads told her she was supposed to like it, but she just couldn't get over the bitter lemon-lime flavoring.

Suddenly, Jack let out a laugh and Betty's head shot up. She raised her eyebrows and waited for Jack to explain what was so hilarious.

"You really don't have to drink that. You are struggling over there!"

"It's that obvious?" Betty asked, cracking a genuine smile for the first time since they'd sat down.

"Let me go get you something else. I feel awful," Jack offered.

"No, that's not necessary. I can't stay too long anyway."

"This didn't really go the way I hoped it would," Jack said with a sigh.

"How did you hope this would go?"

"I don't know. I just thought we'd get along and start from there."

"That's your starting point, but what's your finish line?"

"I'll leave that up to you."

Betty's cheeks were flushed again but for an entirely different reason. Her mind was racing, and she didn't know what she had hoped to get out of her encounter with Jack, either. A free soda? Was that rude to admit? Was that even true?

"I think I should get going. I need to change Joe and get dinner started," Betty said.

"Are you sure?" Jack asked with an unfounded glimmer of hope in his voice.

"I am. Thanks for the TaB."

Betty slipped out of the booth and started walking towards the door with Joe.

"You're going to keep this between you and Mommy, right Joe? Daddy doesn't need to know about this," she whispered to Joe as Jack came running up behind her.

"Let me at least hold the door for you."

"Such a gentleman. Thanks again."

"Next time I'll get the right drink," Jack said as Betty shook her head, slipped past him, and headed home.

Betty found herself almost running home, despite the heat. Something, maybe regret, guilt, intuition, or a combination of it all, made her want to be home with her husband. A sly smile crossed her face as she turned towards her parents' home instead of her own. When she reached the door, she was relieved to find her mother home by herself.

"Hi honey, what are you doing here?" her mother asked as she reached down and swooped Joe into her arms.

"I was wondering if you'd be able to keep Joe tonight."

"Why? Is everything ok?"

"Yes, everything's good. It's just really hot and he's uncomfortable in our stuffy little apartment," Betty explained.

"Of course he can stay! What kind of grandmother says no to a sleepover with her grandbaby?"

"Thanks! I'll come back first thing tomorrow morning, ok?"

"No rush! Are you leaving so quickly?"

"Yeah, I need to do a little cleaning up before Harry gets home tonight. You should have everything you need in the diaper bag."

Walking home, alone, was exactly the kind of break Betty needed. She felt guilty that she had gone out with another man while Harry wasn't home. And she hated herself for not savoring every moment she got to spend with Joe, but she needed a break. It hadn't been a particularly hard day, but she had her own thoughts to sort through without having to worry about a baby. Time to herself was a rarity, and Betty planned to soak it all up while she could.

Soaking it all up just meant taking a nap. Betty had good intentions, but she was so tired. Her eyelids were heavy and the dark circles under her eyes were growing more raccoon-like each day. Something had to give, and she did the only thing she could muster the strength to do: pass out face down on her unmade bed.

"BETTY!" Wake up!! Where is Joe?" Harry shouted at her as he shook her awake.

"Huh? What are you talking about?" Betty mumbled in her half-sleeping state.

"My son. Where is he? He's not in his crib, he's not in here with you. The door was open when I got up the stairs. I think someone took him!" Harry said in a panic.

"Calm down," Betty mumbled.

"Calm down? Calm down? Are you for real? I will not calm down!" Harry yelled, punching the wall behind their bed.

Betty's breath quickened as she jumped to the other side of the bed, far from Harry's reach. She steadied herself before trying to reason with him more.

"Yes. Calm down. He's with my parents. I dropped him off this afternoon."

Harry stomped into the kitchen and Betty closed her eyes, hearing ice clink and something being poured into a glass, she knew it was going to be a long night. Harry had already been out drinking, and now he was going to have more. She just wanted a break. She got out of bed and walked over to Harry, hoping to soothe his worries.

"You didn't even thank me," Harry said without even turning around.

"Thank you for what, exactly?"

"The fan. I brought it home this afternoon to surprise you, but you weren't here."

Out of the corner of her eye, Betty noticed a fan sitting in the living room. Selfishly, she wished she had seen that before she fell into bed early, but she shook that thought off. He had done something so perfect, and she'd been off having a soda with a stranger.

"I thought you said we couldn't afford one. What changed?"

"My mind. Don't worry about it."

Betty's mind was racing. She couldn't decide if his glib response infuriated or comforted her. Realistically, she knew she was a little of both. It was great that he'd found a way to give the family what it needed, but if the only thing that had been standing in the way of comfort was Harry's thoughts, that was unacceptable.

XVII.

Betty rubbed her arms and shivered.

"I always hated the heat when I was younger, but I certainly miss it now," Betty said.

Olivia reached up and fidgeted with the air conditioner vents above them.

"Is that better?" she asked.

Betty smiled and nodded. "Don't worry about me, honey. Discomfort lets me know I'm still alive."

Olivia's eyes widened and she let out a little snicker, unsure of how to react.

"You disagree?" Betty asked.

"I don't know. It just seems like a sad way to think about living. I want to be comfortable."

"And so do I but striving for that comfort is living."

Olivia tilted her head to the side and smiled.

"I never thought of it that way. You might be right."

The thought of discomfort, like so many things, brought Olivia right back to Cole.

"I'm really not feeling great about this, Liv," Cole said as he ran a hand over the front of his shirt to flatten some of the wrinkles.

"About what? Your wrinkled shirt? I have an iron."

"You know it's not the shirt!"

Olivia walked over to Cole and ran her hands down the front of his shirt, mimicking his futile attempt to force some of the wrinkles out. He grabbed her wrists and held them against his chest.

"Dinner at your professor's house isn't really how I want to spend a Friday night."

Olivia nodded. "I know, but it won't be the whole night. We'll have plenty of alone time later. I'll make it up to you."

A smile crept over Cole's face as he nodded.

"You better!" he said, pulling Olivia into a firm embrace.

Olivia kissed him gently before pulling away.

"We need to hurry. I don't want to be late."

"It's not class. Don't worry about punctuality."

"Worry and punctuality are two things I can't let go of!" Olivia said with a smile.

"Oh, I know," Cole said. "Are we doing a rideshare or bus?"

"I'm not sure how to get there. It's probably better to use Uber. Door-to-door service."

Cole nodded as Olivia pulled out her phone and requested the ride.

"Ok, it says our driver will be here in fifteen."

"So, then we have a little time," Cole said, raising his eyebrows and glancing over at the bed.

Olivia hesitated for a minute before laughing.

"Later. Definitely later."

"I can't get a little appetizer?" Cole asked teasingly.

Olivia glanced at her phone again and shrugged as she stepped closer to him. Wrapping her arms around him felt safe. It was easy.

Cole’s hands ran softly down her back as she nuzzled his neck. Slowly, he pulled her closer to him and guided her towards the bed without breaking their embrace. Without a word, Cole pushed Olivia onto the bed in front of him. In one swift motion, Cole was straddling her, pushing his body weight onto her. Olivia quietly moaned as he slid his tongue into her mouth. Her hips raised as if to summon him to move closer. Cole reached down, fumbled with Olivia’s jeans, and pulled slowly on her zipper, giving his hand room to slip into the front of her pants. She closed her eyes and bit her lip, moving in rhythm with Cole’s fingers.

With her breath caught in her throat, she reached for Cole’s hand, trying to push him away. Wriggling back from his reach, she took a deep breath and smiled at him.

“I think we should stop for now,” she said with a palpable tone of disappointment.

Cole reached for her again, playfully refusing to take her denial seriously. She leaned forward and kissed him longingly before slowly separating her lips from his.

"Save room for the main course," Olivia whispered as she pulled away and looked at her phone.

"Appetizers can turn into main courses, you know," Cole teased.

"Not tonight. Tonight, we splurge — appetizer, entree, and dessert! But the driver is at the end of the street. Let's get outside."

Cole let out a disappointed groan. "Ok. Let's get this over with so we can get back to more important matters."

Olivia ran her fingers through her hair.

"Hi! Are you here for Olivia?"

"Yeah," the driver responded.

"Monosyllabic driver, my favorite kind!" Cole whispered in Olivia's ear. She jabbed him with her elbow, hoping the driver hadn't heard him.

The two slid into the back seat of the sedan, making knowing eye contact as they recognized the pungent odor of freshly smoked marijuana. With every bump they hit, Cole pulled her closer to him and Olivia smiled, resting her head on his shoulder. Her leg bounced nervously up and down, and Cole reached over and firmly placed his hand on her thigh. She nuzzled closer to him, but her bouncing legs kept her from enjoying the close ride with him.

Cole glanced over at her out of the corner of his eye and let out a ragged breath.

“Hey! We had a little appetizer before we left, and there’s a big main course, and by ‘big’ I mean you're going to be stuffed before it's over," Cole said with a smile.

Olivia laughed a little. "What's your point?"

"How about we consider this an amuse-bouche?" he suggested.

Shaking her head, Olivia scrunched her nose in disbelief.

"Isn't that the same as an appetizer?"

"Is it? I'm not up on fancy culinary terms." Cole shrugged.

"Or is that supposed to be a palate cleanser? I can't remember," Olivia wondered aloud.

"That's what I was going for! I was saying we can enjoy this dumb dinner as a little break so that we are refreshed and eager for what's to come."

"You're always eager," Olivia said, raising her eyebrows at Cole.

"For you, yes."

The car seemed to be slowing down, and their attention shifted to the windows. With no idea what Professor Jenkins's house looked like, Olivia felt like she was flying over an unfamiliar city, taking in all the scenery from a window seat and pointing to places she thought were important even though she had no idea.

The car lurched to a stop, and Olivia looked out the window, grasping Cole's hand a little tighter.

"This is it?" Cole asked.

Olivia shrugged. "I guess so."

In front of them, a small ranch with chipping white paint and a two-car garage beckoned. As they started to walk up to the front door, Olivia noticed children's toys scattered throughout the yard. An upside-down bicycle with a broken chain sat on the porch, waiting for someone to fix it. Helmets, balls, jump ropes, and even a skateboard littered the yard as if a toy box had exploded, leaving a mess in its wake.

The sound of children laughing crept through the front door.

"Looks like we've made it to the party!" Cole joked.

"Maybe this isn't the right house," Olivia said.

Just then, the front door swung open, and Professor Jenkins was standing in front of them.

"Welcome! Come on in."

The couple walked past the toys in their path and followed the professor into his living room.

"Dad!! Who are these people?"

"Why are they here?"

Loud questions from little voices.

Professor Jenkins shook his head and crouched down in front of his children.

"These are my guests. We've talked about this before. Guests should be welcomed into our home and met with smiles. Do you want to learn their names?"

The kids looked at the floor and nodded slowly.

"This is Olivia. She's one of my best students! And that's her boyfriend... I'm sorry, what's your name?"

"I'm Cole."

"Ah, Cole. Sorry, I forgot that."

"It's fine. I don't even think we've met before, so it'd be kinda weird if you knew it."

Olivia could feel the heat rising to her cheeks. How could he be so rude? They were guests and Professor Jenkins was being so kind.

She caught the professor's eye and mouthed, *I'm sorry*. He smiled and winked at her. The embarrassed flushing of her cheeks was still there, but now it was different. Did embarrassed and flattered feel the same? That hadn't been her experience in the past, but then again there hadn't been many times in her life when Olivia was flattered.

"Right. Ok, well nice to meet you, Cole."

"You too, Professor."

"Ah! Let's lose the 'Professor' nonsense for tonight, ok? I'm Charles, or Charlie, whichever you prefer. And this little guy here is Tommy." Lifting a tiny girl with blonde curls into his arms, "And this is our little princess, Veronica," he said.

"How about a tour?" Charles asked.

"Sounds great Profess—" Olivia caught herself before she could get the whole word out. "Charles!" she laughed.

"Doesn't that just feel better coming off your tongue?" he asked with a smile.

Cole linked arms with Olivia, who was starting to laugh nervously. "I'm here. Just relax," he whispered in her ear.

She let out a slow breath and nodded, steeling herself for the night ahead. The noisy, disheveled house was not at all what she had imagined, but when Olivia was honest with herself, it all made him seem a little more human. As they followed him through the house, the toys, the worn-down and broken crayons on the floor, even the half-eaten peanut butter and jelly sandwich on the coffee table, seemed to leave Charles unbothered; as if anyone would believe the mess belonged exactly where it was.

"Am I having a stroke, or does it smell like burnt toast?" Cole whispered to Olivia.

"SHIT!"

"Ooooo Mommy said a bad word!" Tommy said.

"Not a bad word, a grown-up word, buddy," Charles explained to his son.

"I better go check on her," he said as he hurried toward the kitchen.

"This means we can have pizza!" Tommy said with a knowing grin.

Olivia started to laugh as Cole high-fived Tommy, celebrating at the prospect of pizza. The pizza celebration was drowned out by a muffled argument happening in the next room. Angry tones, slamming drawers, and exasperated sighs accompanied the smoke as it emanated from the kitchen. They hadn't even met yet, but Olivia was sure Charles's wife hated her. Even if she had no idea about the rendezvous in his office, an unwelcome guest adding to the stress of dinnertime with two young children had to be upsetting.

Charles came walking out of the kitchen, holding paper menus for local pizza places.

"Do you guys mind pizza?" he asked, shrugging.

"Mind pizza? Does anyone ever say no to pizza?" Cole asked, offering a fist bump to Tommy, who reared back and met Cole's fist with all the power his little arm could muster.

"I think the better question is, what's with the pizza brochures?"

Just then Rachel, Charles's wife, came walking into the living room. Her face was flushed, her cheeks were tearstained, and her eyes were bloodshot, but she greeted them with a smile.

"Olivia. Cole. This is my wife, Rachel," Charles said, wrapping an arm around her waist and pulling her close to his side, and kissing her cheek.

"Nice to meet you," they said in unison.

"Sorry about burning dinner. But did I just hear you call the takeout menus 'pizza brochures'?"

Olivia's eyes darted between Cole and Charles, hoping one of them would give her an out. She bit her bottom lip and could feel her heart rate quickening.

"Next thing you know she's going to call us boomers," Rachel said to Charles, shaking her head.

"Umm... well, I mean, it was a joke," she said.

"Wait! You aren't boomers?" Cole said in the most earnest tone he could manage.

Olivia let out a deep breath and felt the tension leave her shoulders. Cole really was going to keep her from getting swept away in her thoughts.

"Gen X, actually, but you millennials think anyone older than you has one foot in the grave!" Rachel retorted.

"Oh, ouch! We aren't millennials! Gen Z here," Olivia said, smiling.

"Ok, I have an important question to ask. This will make or break our night," Charles said.

Olivia looked at Cole and smiled nervously. He smiled and nodded, reassuring her that no matter what, the night was going to be fine.

"Pineapple on pizza or not?" Charles asked.

"Dad! I want cheese!" Tommy said.

He looked down at his son and nodded. "I know. Don't worry. We'll get more than one pizza, ok?"

"Dude! Does that mean you don't like pineapple on your pizza?" Cole asked him.

"I only like cheese!" Tommy said, stomping his feet.

Cole put his hands up in defeat.

"You don't know what you're missing little dude."

"One cheese pizza and one pineapple and bacon?" Charles asked.

"Sounds good."

Charles left the room, putting space between himself and his overexcited children, to order the pizza. Olivia's eyes followed him as he walked into the next room as if ordering pizza was the most important thing he had ever been tasked with. Olivia found his zeal for everything, no matter how minuscule or monotonous, to be refreshing. For Cole, it seemed natural to be lackadaisical and careless unless something truly was deemed important. Sure, he took school seriously, and sometimes it felt as if he would rather study than spend time with her, but for the most part he didn't act as if he cared. If she was being honest with herself, she'd have to admit she was more like Cole than Charles, and that difference excited her.

Almost as quickly as he had left the room, Charles returned, smiling, and announced that the pizza would be there within the hour.

"In the meantime, Olivia, should we discuss your questions from class? We can go to my office."

Olivia's mind was spinning. What was he talking about? What questions? Why not just enjoy dinner? There was no way that didn't look at least a little suspicious, but Charles didn't seem to care.

"I mean if no one minds us leaving them for a few minutes," Olivia said with a shrug.

"I'll keep Rachel and the kids entertained. Go. Take care of your problem," Cole said.

Olivia's eyes darted between Cole and Rachel. She wasn't sure if it was the best idea to be alone with Charles while her boyfriend and his wife were there. As the word wife crossed her mind, she second-guessed herself. He had a wife. He had two adorable kids running around. He had a stable, albeit messy, home. He had a lot to lose. Why would he risk all of that for her? Plus, she had Cole to think about.

Despite her hesitation, she got up and started to follow Charles out of the living room. She met Rachel's eyes as she walked past. There was no way to know for certain, but Olivia felt like the look was begging her not to do anything but study in the office. It was a sad, knowing stare. Were the rumors true? Had he done this before?

Walking behind Charles, her heart started racing. Her mind was spiraling, and Cole couldn't save her from this one. He opened the door to his office and the smell of leather and peppermint spilled out.

"After you," Charles said, motioning for Olivia to enter the office.

A tight smile crossed her face and Olivia let out a deep breath. His office was pristine. There were no crumbs on the floor, no toys, not even a paper out of place on his desk.

"No kids allowed in here," he said, almost reading Olivia's mind.

"I couldn't tell," she quipped.

"Yeah, I know the house is a mess, but things have been a little crazy around here lately. We've been remodeling the upstairs and may have bit off a little more than we can chew. Handy, I am not!"

"I'm used to dorm rooms; mess isn't anything new."

"Hopefully I've grown a little since I was living in a dorm."

Charles took a seat behind his desk and folded his hands. Olivia was motionless in the doorway. Did he expect her to join him behind the desk? Did Cole and Rachel suspect anything? Would his children come looking for him? There were so many unknowns. A tinge of excitement flowed through her. Being around Charles was exciting. It was dangerous, wrong, exhilarating.

"So, Ms. Standford, should we pick up where we left off last time?"

Olivia bit her bottom lip, feeling the heat rise to her cheeks, her heart racing. She took a small step towards him, letting out a ragged breath. Did he want what she thought he did?

"Where were we?" she asked with a knowing smile.

"Discussing the test. We didn't get much done."

As quickly as it had appeared, her smile was gone. What was he talking about? Had he really invited her to dinner to discuss a test? Had she done something wrong? Her thought tornado was back in full force.

"Oh, yeah. I've looked over my notes again. I'll probably be ok."

"Yeah, probably. You're a bright student."

Olivia's eyes darted around the room; she couldn't let him see her disappointment. She had clearly misread the situation.

"Thanks."

"Olivia, I think you understand the moral quandaries that we've been talking about in class. You know all about Piaget and Kohlberg, and the ways morality grows and develops on a wider scale."

She knew he was right, and that was what they were discussing, but it seemed to be a little too close to home to be addressing morality.

"I do. Morality is absolute and static," she stated flatly.

"What? No! Not even close. Have you forgotten all about Kohlberg's theory of moral development?"

"Well, I'm a woman. I'm stuck somewhere around his third level of morality because I care about the welfare of other people," Olivia said, trying to hide her smile.

Charles reached his hand out to her, summoning her to join him behind his desk. She walked over and stood in front of him for a moment before leaning back against his desk.

"You had me for a minute there," he laughed.

As he ran his finger gently up her arm, he glanced at the door and let out a sigh. Olivia's eyes followed his, afraid for a moment that someone was going to walk in and find them.

"I know exactly where we left off last time, and, as far as I'm concerned, it never happened," he said.

His hand slinked away from her, his fingertips trailing a little longer.

Olivia squinted; it wasn't the rejection she had expected.

"Daddy!! The pizza is here! Hurry!" Tommy's little voice shouted from behind the door.

Charles smiled, and Olivia let out a deep breath before heading back to the living room to rejoin Cole and Rachel.

"You're going to ace this test, Ms. Standford!" Charles said loud enough for everyone to hear. Olivia thought that made things even more suspicious, but then again literally nothing had happened, so why did she feel so guilty?

Charles walked straight to Rachel and kissed her forehead before reaching for the pizza box. Rachel backed away from Charles and looked over at Olivia, who smiled in return. She could almost feel Rachel's disdain for her. Charles grabbed a couple of slices of pizza for himself and sat down on the couch.

"I hope you don't mind; we're not fancy. We eat in the living room."

"I'm not even sure why we have a dining room table at my house. We only use it on holidays," Cole said.

While the men were digging into the pizza, Rachel was cutting up slices for Tommy and Veronica. Olivia grabbed a slice and sat crossed-legged on the floor between Cole and Tommy, who seemed to have become fast friends. She caught Charles's eye and he smiled and winked at her, almost as if to say they had gotten away with something. Maybe that was just in her head. She leaned over and laid her head on Cole's shoulder before whispering in his ear. The smile that crossed his lips gave away their secret, and Olivia couldn't have been happier about that. If she was going to be whispering sweet nothings in one man's ear, it seemed unlikely that she had just finished doing anything with another man, right? She was hoping. Then again, maybe Rachel thought she was some oversexed slutty coed.

Cole put his arm around her shoulder and pulled her closer to whisper, "It's ok. You're ok. This is going well, and it's almost time for our entrée."

Olivia smiled. He was a good guy. He was starting to check off more of her boxes. Seeing him with Tommy made her have more faith that he'd eventually be a great dad. But she knew she was getting ahead of herself. He was just being on his best behavior because he knew how important this dinner was to her.

"Want me to request the Uber? We're a little far from most people so it might take a while," Cole said.

Olivia just nodded and took a bite of her pizza. She was ready to be alone with Cole again. Dinner with the professor and his family wasn't something she wanted to do again. She should have known she'd spend most of the night stuck in her own thoughts, finding reasons for everyone to hate her.

"Red wine or white?" Charles asked.

"Oh, no thanks, we don't want to overstay our welcome," Olivia said.

"Nonsense! A dinner party isn't complete without at least one drink."

Olivia and Cole exchanged looks, and Cole reached for his phone to cancel the Uber.

"You're right. We're good with whatever, so long as you don't card us," Cole said.

Charles laughed and walked to the kitchen for a bottle of sauvignon blanc, a bottle of apple juice, and some glasses. He carefully poured apple juice for the kids before moving on to the wine.

He raised his glass and bent down to clink glasses with his kids.

"Cheers, Daddy!" the two little voices said in unison.

"Cheers!"

Rachel grabbed the kids' plates and then reached for Olivia's and Cole's plates.

"Oh, thank you. Can I help you clean up?" Olivia asked.

"It was pizza. Don't worry about it," Rachel said, smiling.

"Right," Olivia said with a defeated laugh.

Charles had disappeared just in time for Rachel to be left with the trash from dinner. Just as fast as he had slipped away, he peered around the corner and called to Olivia.

"I was thinking about your feminist take on Kohlberg, and I think you might like this rebuttal," he said, handing her a book. "Gilligan calls the theory out for its primarily male take on things. Interesting read."

"Ok, will this be on the test?" Olivia asked with a wink.

"Ha. Consider it supplemental reading. Do it, don't. I just thought you'd like it."

"Thanks. I'll definitely read it and get this back to you."

Charles smiled. "Stop by the office when you're done, and we'll discuss it."

"Can we stop all of this shop talk and enjoy the night?" Rachel asked, shuffling a deck of cards she had pulled out of a side table drawer.

Without a word, Charles grabbed the cards from her hands and started shuffling, and signaled for everyone else to sit around the coffee table.

"Everyone knows how to play euchre?" Charles asked.

Cole and Olivia looked at each other and laughed. Olivia shook her head.

"I guess that's what you get when you're at a party with a couple of boomers! I was hoping we were going to play kings," Cole said with a laugh.

"What? I've never even heard of that game," Rachel said.

"Pretty sure it's a drinking game, Rach. We'll teach these kids how to play euchre. A real card game."

Before anyone could object, he started dealing cards as he explained the rules of the game. He looked across the table, and smiled at Olivia, who was tilting her head, trying to understand what he meant as he quickly threw out phrases like "making the trump," "order it up," "I assist," and "crossing it."

"All right, so everyone understands?" Charles asked confidently, ready to start playing.

"Can we just play go fish or something? You lost me before you even started," Cole said.

Olivia bit her bottom lip, trying not to laugh.

"Let's give their game a try instead," Rachel suggested. "It probably has fewer rules."

Charles shook his head, adamantly against letting go of the idea of playing the game Cole had suggested.

"It's a drinking game. Do you want to get blackout drunk with a couple of college kids? Grow up!" he admonished Rachel.

Rachel looked down at the table and shook her head. "How was I supposed to know that?" she asked softly.

Olivia's heart was racing, feeling the same pang of discomfort she felt when her parents would fight in front of her and she couldn't get away from them. She reached into her pocket and pulled out her phone.

Ready? she texted to Cole.

Def, he responded, and followed up with a screenshot of an already-requested Uber.

Rachel was drinking her wine as if the goal was to get drunk, and Olivia joined her, quickly downing her own glass of wine before reaching for Cole's and finishing his as well.

"Our women are outdrinking us," Charles quipped.

"It happens," Cole said with a shrug.

"Next time, we'll break out the hard stuff."

A tight smile came across Cole's face as he nodded.

"Our Uber is here. I have some work I need to get done, so we have to get back to campus."

"Thanks for dinner. It was great to meet your family," Olivia said.

"Great to meet your boyfriend. Thanks for coming!" Charles said.

The couple walked to the door without even noticing that Tommy was following close behind Cole.

"Hey! I thought we were going to play Legos!" he said, pouting.

"Oh, sorry little dude. Next time, ok?"

"Next time? Like tomorrow?"

"Not tomorrow, but we'll do it soon. Maybe your dad will play with you."

"He never plays with me."

"Tommy! Leave them alone. They have to go home now. Don't be a pest," Charles yelled at him.

Cole reached out his fist for Tommy to bump and promised him he'd play next time.

Olivia and Cole got into the Uber, alone at last. The bumpy road back to reality gave Olivia time to rest her head on Cole and feel steady again.

"Ready for the main course?" she whispered to Cole.

"I'm starving!" he said.

He rubbed her thigh as they drove closer to campus, which felt hours away from where they were.

"Your professor was kind of scary."

"Scary? Do you mean intimidating? He's super smart, so that's always how I feel."

"No. Scary. Didn't you hear the yelling in the kitchen when Rachel burned the dinner? And then poor little Tommy? Dude is scary."

XVIII.

Betty shifted in her seat and let out a soft sigh. Olivia looked over at her, unsure if she needed to stretch or was bored of Olivia's story.

"Are you ok?" she asked.

"Oh yes, I just have little tolerance for angry men around vulnerable children," Betty responded, tilting her head to the side.

Olivia's heart was beating faster. Maybe she didn't want to share that part of the story with Betty. Perfect stranger or not, her opinion was starting to matter to her.

"You don't have any experience with men like that, do you?" Olivia asked.

Betty let out a ragged breath and nodded slowly.

"That's a tough question."

"Yeah, sorry. I don't mean to pry." Olivia's cheeks flushed with embarrassment. She wasn't typically the type to put anyone else in an awkward situation that she knew she'd hate to be in.

Betty shook her head and leaned back. "I said tough, not intrusive."

The two women sat in silence, both lost in thought before Betty was taken right back to her run-down apartment with Harry.

Several days had passed since she and Harry fought about buying a new fan, and Betty wanted nothing more than for him to let it go. She was ready for the fight to be over. She made his breakfast and lunch every day like clockwork and handed them off with a smile, and she received only a rough peck on the cheek in return. There seemed to be nothing she could do to apologize and show how grateful she was that he had given in. A heatwave wasn't what she had expected to cause the first major rift of their marriage. New Englanders should anticipate extreme weather, be it heat waves or blizzards. It wasn't anything new for either of them. Dealing with the discomfort together, on the other hand, was a brand-new challenge.

"I don't know why Daddy is so angry, buddy," Betty whispered to Joe as she bounced him on her lap, hoping to get him down for an early nap so she could get the housework done without interruption. Fortunately, Joe was more cooperative than his father and fell asleep in Betty's arms in no time at all.

She laid him gently in his bassinet and tiptoed into the kitchen to get started on the breakfast dishes. It seemed like that was her life these days: cooking, cleaning, rocking a baby, and repeating it all over again. It wasn't exactly what she had imagined her life would be. But here she was, barely pushing back against the tide that seemed to be pulling her out to a sea of monotony. Like clockwork, Betty heard rustling coming from Joe's bassinet. Joe was more committed to the schedule than his mother and he knew it was time to leave the apartment.

Taking afternoon walks around the neighborhood, pushing Joe in his baby carriage, she couldn't help but hope she would run into Jack. Her mind would flitter between wanting to see him, hoping she never saw him again, and imagining every scenario possible in either direction. What would life be like without Harry? And should she even be thinking about it? They just had a baby! This was her life now and she needed to get over the idea that there was going to be excitement and romance in her future. He had given her all of that with their cemetery rendezvous while they were dating. Now, it was time for her to be a wife and a mother. That meant it was time to embrace the monotony. That didn't mean her imagination had to die, though.

"Do you see the birds, Joe?" she said softly as she crouched down next to the carriage.

She wasn't sure if he had any idea what she was saying, but she knew she should talk to him. Talking had to be good. She wanted Joe to be smart and well-spoken so he would have every opportunity to get out of run-down apartments and avoid dead-end jobs. A smile spread across her face, and Betty started walking towards her parents' house, just a couple of blocks away.

Before she could even knock, the door swung open.

"Hi, honey! What a surprise! What are you doing here?" her mother asked.

"We were just out for a walk, and I thought we'd stop by."

Without a word, her mother scooped Joe up out of the carriage and started talking in a high-pitched voice. Her words were barely words to Betty. The baby talk, "goo-goo ga-ga" nonsense that grandparents and strangers so often used to talk to babies always drove Betty a little crazy, but she never said anything. Being sure that her mother would barely notice she'd left the room, never mind miss her, Betty started towards her old bedroom. Of course, her parents had changed things around; she was married with a baby now, so it wasn't really her room anymore. But she couldn't help but hope they had left a few things untouched.

As she turned the doorknob, she knew she shouldn't get her hopes up, but there was one thing she really wanted to find. No matter how many times her parents tried to convince her that she was too old for certain books, Betty could never part with the ones she loved. For some reason on their walk that afternoon, she was overcome with the need to share her love of these books with her baby boy. He may not understand them immediately, and it was entirely possible that he wouldn't even enjoy them, but she had to give it a shot. Sometimes reading those books, long after she was the target audience, helped her relax.

Sitting in a box in the back of the closet, she found exactly what she was looking for. She pulled the box out and sat on the floor, pouring over the pages of A.A. Milne's *Winnie-the-Pooh* and Beatrix Potter's *The Tale of Peter Rabbit.* Slowly she was stacking book after book next to her, imagining the peaceful nights she could have reading these stories to Joe. He would surely grow to love them, too.

"I knew you'd be looking for those," her mother said softly as she crouched down beside her.

"I thought you'd throw them away."

"Never. I knew those books were important to you and you'd want to share them someday."

"Thanks, Mom."

Her mother just smiled and nodded as she picked up the piles of books and stacked them in paper grocery bags.

"They belong in a home with a child. Take them with you."

Betty looked over at the clock hanging in the hallway and jumped up in a hurry. 3:30. She had to get home and dinner started.

"Where's Joe?"

"Your father is playing with him downstairs. They finished early at the shop today."

Betty's eyes widened and she scooped up the paper bags, one in each arm, and ran down to get Joe.

"I'll take the rest of the books next time, ok? I have to go."

"Sure. What's the rush?"

"If Dad's home, that means Harry is too and he's going to be expecting dinner to be cooking," she said in a panic.

"He's probably at the bar with the rest of the guys," her father assured her.

Her mother shook her head as she watched Betty place Joe back in the carriage and head for the door.

"Say goodbye, Joe."

Juggling the bags full of books and the handles of the baby carriage wasn't enough to slow Betty down. She was determined to get home and get dinner started before it prompted an even bigger fight with Harry. The closer they got to the apartment the more Betty found herself hoping, for the first time ever, that Harry really was out drinking. She needed more time to get ready for him to be home. Without the smell of dinner cooking, he was sure to accuse her of being lazy, unloving, and worthless. She wasn't ready for any of that.

XIX.

"I bet your son loved being read to," Olivia said.

"He did." A smile came across Betty's face, and she looked off as if she were watching things play out in real time "Of course, he made me read the same books so often he managed to memorize them. I remember Harry truly believing he was a genius, reading full books at the age of two."

"That's amazing! What gave him away?"

Betty laughed a little. "That would have been when the power went out and we could barely see our hands in front of our faces, but there was our little man, reading away as if *Curious George* was illuminated."

"This is George. He lived in Africa. He was a good little monkey and always very curious."

The room was so dark, Betty's eyes were still struggling to adjust to the sudden blackout; yet somehow her toddler was reading. Through the darkness, Betty caught Harry's gaze and shook her head. Sure, she had read that book to Joe every time she put him down for a nap that he wanted no part of, with his eyelids looking heavier with each passing moment, but there was no way a boy his age could possibly memorize so much, right? Lo and behold, that was exactly what he did.

"One day he saw the man in the yellow hat!" Joe said, breathlessly.

"Was the man afraid of George?" Betty asked. "Because I would be afraid if I saw a monkey roaming around, wouldn't you?"

Joe slammed the paperback book down with as much force as his little muscles could muster and let out a loud sigh.

"No, Mommy! The man in the yellow hat wanted to take him home." Joe shook his head and sat silently for a minute. "Daddy, do you want a monkey like George?"

Harry didn't miss a beat, scooped Joe up, and replied, "I already have you, little monkey!"

Before he could say another word, Harry had Joe hanging upside down over his arms, climbing and begging to be flipped over again and again. Betty sat there listening to the laughter echoing around her and closed her eyes, knowing that Harry had everything under control for once. Almost as quickly as she had faded off to sleep, the power was back on and their little apartment was buzzing. The light was blinding, and the radio felt far too loud and grating, despite the harmony of Peter, Paul, and Mary singing Joe's new favorite song.

"Lived by the sea / And frolicked in the autumn mist in a land called Honah Lee."

"Puff!" Joe exclaimed, jumping onto Betty's lap as if he were making sure she knew her break was over.

XX.

"Aww! I remember that song. My parents loved playing Peter, Paul, and Mary around the house when I was little."

Betty nodded, "Joe couldn't get enough of them. Little boys, dragons, and all things untamed defined my life for a while."

"At least it sounds like Harry could keep up with him and give you a break sometimes."

Betty scrunched her nose and bit her bottom lip. There was no denying Harry had been a great father, and Joe loved him, but even after all the years that had gone by, she wasn't ready to give him credit, never mind forgiveness.

"He was a good father," Betty said flatly.

Olivia tilted her head and asked, "But that was it?"

"Oh, well things aren't always so..." Betty paused, searching for the right words.

"Binary?" Olivia said.

"Black and white," Betty said.

Olivia just smiled to herself and nodded. There was something oddly familiar about the way Betty had said that. Maybe it had been her own grandmother who had tried to tell her life wasn't that simple, but Olivia tended to zone out those life lessons when they came from someone so close to home.

"I wish I had listened to my grandmother about things not being cut and dry. I'm always looking for concrete answers in life, but it's not like life hasn't tried to teach me that on its own," Olivia said.

Betty nodded and looked at Olivia with a reassuring smile.

"Life tries its best to teach us, but not even the best among us listen all the time," Betty said.

"So true."

"I'm sure you've experienced that, with or without your grandmother reminding you," Betty said with a little snicker.

"More than once," Olivia relented.

After a moment of hesitation, Olivia jumped back into her story.

There hadn't been a solid reason for Olivia to stop by Professor Jenkins's office that afternoon, but that hadn't stopped her in the past, so why would it this time? Of course, the guilt of having actually met his wife and kids weighed heavy on her mind, but then, if she were being honest, that was his problem, not hers. Her trouble came in a less legally binding form of commitment with Cole. And Cole was the reason she felt she needed to go talk to the professor. The idea of hurting him crushed her; he was an integral part of her daily life. As for her professor, Olivia needed to be sure they were on the same page about where they were taking their affair. Was it over? Did they each have big choices to make? Could things stay the same?

Shade from overhanging red dogwood trees that lined the street was spotty at best, but that wasn't what Olivia loved about those trees. A beautiful, short-lived splash of color decorating the campus helped Olivia stay present in the moment, and she was careful not to rush to Professor Jenkins's office and miss the sheer beauty of the nature around her. She took one final deep breath, taking in the floral scents that filled the street, and headed into the building, ready for any way the conversation with Professor Jenkins could go.

Olivia climbed the stairs to his office and took a deep breath before turning the corner, but her heart stopped when she found the door open and a woman sitting behind the desk. At first glance, Olivia believed there was another student sitting in the professor's chair, her head down, showing only a messy bun and hunched shoulders. As she stepped gingerly into the office, the woman looked up and smiled.

"Olivia! So nice to see you!"

Olivia's eyes widened, her legs froze, and she flashed a smile. Not a smile that lit up the room, but one that offered a friendly greeting to Rachel.

"Hi!" Olivia said, with as much forced enthusiasm as she could muster. "I thought I was in time for office hours. I don't mean to interrupt."

"Oh, no. You are on time. Charlie just stepped out with the kids. He'll be right back," Rachel explained.

"Ok, thanks."

Olivia glanced down at the rug, trying to find an escape. She edged closer to the dark wood-paneled wall and focused her attention on the floor. The crimson and gold patterns flowing through the rug were distracting, but as much as she tried to just disappear into the office décor, she couldn't hide from the one woman she had reason to hide from.

"From what I hear, you're a fabulous student. What could you possibly need help with?" Rachel asked.

Olivia let out a little laugh. Yes, she was a pretty good student, but there were extracurricular matters at hand.

"I'm a bit of a perfectionist, I guess," Olivia shrugged.

"Mommy!!!" a little voice screeched from the stairwell. "Mommy! Look at what Daddy let us get!"

Tommy and Veronica came bursting into the office shaking bags of M&M's and bottles of orange soda.

"Wow! That's a lot of sugar, Daddy!" Rachel said with a sneer as she glared at Charles.

"I think they'll be fine. They promised to drink all their milk at dinner tonight," Charles said.

Rachel let out an exaggerated breath and tore open the candy for the kids.

"Ms. Standford! I'm sorry things are a little crazy here right now. You remember Rachel, right?" Charles asked.

"Of course," Olivia said.

"What can I do for you? Questions about the reading? Or do you just want to chat?"

Olivia shifted her weight from one foot to the other and fidgeted with a bracelet. "A little bit of everything," she replied, scrunching her nose.

Rachel and the kids walked out into the hall, closing the office door behind them.

Charles stared at the door for a moment, relaxed his shoulders, and tilted his head while waggling his eyebrows at Olivia. Her heart started to beat faster as her eyes met his, and he tapped his hand on his desk, beckoning her forward. Much like a well-trained dog, she obeyed and awaited her treat. He draped his arms over her shoulders and moved in closer, kissing her gently on the forehead. Olivia shifted away from him and flashed a nervous smile.

"Your wife and kids are out there. And that's not why I'm here, but I'll come back later," Olivia whispered as she slipped off the desk and out the door before he could argue.

Closing the door behind her, Olivia leaned against it, closed her eyes, and looked up to the ceiling, letting out a ragged breath.

"Olivia!" Tommy and Veronica shouted in unison.

She looked down at the kids and smiled. "Hi guys! How's the candy?"

"All gone!"

"That was fast. You guys must have been hungry."

"No, I just love chocolate," Veronica said in a matter-of-fact tone that sounded far beyond her years.

"Me too, kiddo. Me too," Olivia laughed. "I know a place around here that has delicious chocolate milkshakes. I might have to go get one while I do my homework."

Veronica's eyes widened at the mention of milkshakes being nearby. Olivia caught Rachel's eye and knew right away that she was not impressed with the mention of even more sugar in front of her already hyperactive children.

"They have amazing coffee there, too," Olivia said. "Today might not be the best day for milkshakes." She hoped that helped the predicament she'd put herself in just mentioning the milkshakes.

"Well, I could go for a coffee and some grown-up company if you have time," Rachel said.

Olivia froze, not sure of what to do. Wasn't the awkward dinner party enough interaction with the wife of a man she was having an illicit relationship with? On the other hand, she wondered if being close to Rachel would keep any possible suspicion at bay.

"I never say no to coffee," Olivia said. "Follow me, it's not too far."

XXI.

"Never talk about chocolate with a little one unless you are willing to face the wrath of an angry parent," Betty said with a laugh.

"Yeah, well, live and learn, huh?" Olivia replied.

"Too bad we can't get milkshakes on the plane," Betty joked.

"So true! Forget the mile-high club I'd rather have a mile-high milkshake!"

The women's laughter carried through the plane cabin, eliciting some grumbles and stares from some of the more subdued passengers. Quiet was never a skill Betty had managed to master. It wasn't that she was the type of woman who gossiped and chatted with everyone she met, but her mother always told her that her voice carried. Betty would roll her eyes and ignore her mother's criticism.

A man across the aisle from the women shook his head in disapproval and let out a deep sigh as he mumbled, "They're never going to shut up!" under his breath.

"I've had people telling me to shut up forever, and you're right, it's not going to happen," Betty quipped, making Olivia laugh even more.

The man just grumbled, put his earbuds in, and turned towards the window.

"One of the greatest skills all moms have is understanding the snide comments made under breaths," Betty explained with a smile.

"Do you have any daughters? I feel like girls are more apt to do that to their mothers," Olivia said.

Betty's eyes lit up as she nodded. "I have one, Patricia. We called her Patty Cakes when she was really small," Betty explained, "but she hated it by the time she was in school, so it didn't stick around too long."

"Is she close in age to her brother?" Olivia asked.

"There are four years between Patty and Joe, and then three between Patty and Ricky."

"Wow, you had a full house, huh?"

"Harry would've had three more if I let him."

Olivia snickered and shook her head at Betty. Without missing a beat, Betty jumped right back into her story.

It had been two years since Joe was born, and Betty had been going stir-crazy for almost as long. Sure, there was a lot for her to do with a new husband, a home to tend to, and a toddler in tow, but it wasn't enough. The young girl who had dreamed of a big life became a young woman trapped in a shoebox apartment with nothing more than a shoestring budget and time.

"I heard that the printing company downtown is hiring," Betty said to Harry as he sipped his coffee.

"I have a job," he said flatly.

Betty closed her eyes and took a deep breath. As if on cue, Joe started to cry from the other room, and Betty slipped away to comfort him and restore her resolve. Calming Joe was a skill that came easier to Betty than she had ever believed possible. She knew what each distinct cry meant, and more importantly, she knew he was running the show. Unfortunately, thinking of ways to convince Harry that two incomes were better than one was tricky. Even a day out at her parents' home resulted in anxiety over uncooked or late dinners. Convincing him that by leaving the house every day she would be improving their lives was something she knew would take some effort.

"Oh, I'll need some money today," Betty mentioned nonchalantly.

"What for? You just went grocery shopping two days ago."

"We need more than just food, you know."

Harry furrowed his brow and shook his head.

"No kidding. But what do you need today?"

Betty moved closer to Harry and ran her fingers down his arm.

"Joe needs some new clothes. His are getting a little snug."

Harry let out a deep breath and shook his head as he reached for his wallet. He pulled out two ten-dollar bills and dragged them slowly across Betty's chest, looking at her with a sly smile. She placed one hand over the money, and the other behind Harry's neck, drawing him in for a kiss.

"You're going to make my pants a little snug, too," Harry joked as he pulled away.

Betty shrugged and gave him one more quick peck on the lips before he walked towards the front door and headed to work.

With a new plan brewing in her mind, Betty grinned as she scooped Joe up off the living room floor and prepared him for a day out.

"Are you ready to go shopping, Joey?"

She grabbed the diaper bag and swung it over her shoulder before bending down to grab Joe's favorite stuffed animal that would surely keep him quiet in the store. With Joe in his stroller and all the essentials prepared for a day out, Betty headed downtown to Denholmes Department Store. It wasn't going to be the cheapest place to shop; for that, she could have headed to Zayre's.

"Bird!" Joe shouted, pointing to the sky.

"Very good, bud. Can you count the birds while we walk?" Betty asked.

"One."

With the sun shining on a cool spring day, they were sure to see plenty of birds, and Betty knew keeping Joe occupied would give her more time to perfect her plan and come up with a way to convince Harry that two incomes far surpassed one accompanied by consistent but mediocre dinners.

"Two!"

She had made up her mind that Joe was going to get more than what he actually needed. Harry spent a lot of time playing with Joe, but he rarely got him dressed or undressed and changed, so Betty was confident that he would be oblivious to the superfluous nature of her purchase.

"Four!" Joe yelled excitedly.

"What happened to three?" Betty said with a laugh.

Joe tilted his head to the side and scrunched his face, appearing to be deep in thought and confusion.

As she pushed the carriage towards the large revolving door, she noticed it was full of foot traffic from Main Street. Unsure of whom she might run into, she straightened her skirt, put her shoulders back, and walked with purpose into the store.

She stopped just past the front door and scanned a list of departments until she noticed "boys' clothes." Grumbling to herself, Betty pushed the call button for the elevator and leaned down to check on her son.

"Ok, Joe. We need to go to thc third floor. Want to help Mommy push the right button in the elevator?"

Joe nodded excitedly; he loved to push the buttons. Before the elevator doors opened, Betty reached down and unfastened the buckle holding Joe in the seat, but put a hand on his shoulder, telling him not to get up yet. Once the elevator made the familiar dinging sound and the doors slid open Joe was kicking his legs out in anticipation.

"We need to go to level three. Can you find number three?" Betty directed Joe. She lifted him to see the buttons and counted with him.

"One, two, three," they recited together.

Joe pushed the button for level three and Betty placed him back in the stroller, quickly fastening the buckle.

She walked down the aisles, past the home décor that she knew she couldn't buy. Her point wasn't going to be made with indulgent purchases. Betty was set on showing Harry that just providing the bare necessities was something they were struggling to do on one income.

"Aww. Look at these dungarees! You're going to look so handsome in these," Betty said, holding a pair of jeans up in front of Joe as if he could offer an opinion. "Hmm, I think these will fit you for a while. A little big, but that's just room to grow."

After finding the jeans, a few shirts, and a pair of shorts, Joe was getting restless and Betty knew their shopping trip was running on fumes, and it was time to head home. A day of shopping with a toddler wasn't quite as fun as shopping with her friends in high school, although she had a similarly tight budget.

Joe fell asleep on the walk home, giving Betty the chance to lose herself in thought without much interruption. When they reached the house, Betty carefully picked Joe up out of his carriage, and with him in one arm and the shopping bags in the other, she managed to get the door unlocked and slip into the apartment without disrupting Joe's nap. She gingerly placed him in his crib and snuck off to the kitchen to get started on dinner.

Betty washed and peeled potatoes, leaving her fingers red and raw, but there was something serene about peeling vegetables. She wasn't sure if it was the repetitive motion or the rhythmic sound, but it was a task Betty could easily be lost in. Once the potatoes were boiling away on the stovetop, Betty breaded the chicken breast and slipped that into the oven.

"Mmmm! Something smells good," Harry said, walking up behind Betty.

Betty jumped. "Oh you scared me! You're home early," she said.

"Slow day at the shop," he explained.

Harry wrapped his arm around Betty's waist and pulled her in closer to him, kissing her softly.

"We can pick up where we left off this morning," Harry suggested.

Betty leaned into him, running her fingernails gently down his back. She peered up to see Harry biting his bottom lip. He guided her toward the living room and pushed her down onto the couch. She ran her finger over the button of his jeans and smiled up at him as he guided her hand to his zipper and helped her pull it down.

Without a word, Betty unfastened his button and slid her hand down into his jeans. Harry shivered and took a ragged breath as she grasped him gently and freed him from his tight pants. The two fell into a perfect rhythm, Harry's hips thrusting up and Betty meeting each thrust eagerly.

A familiar sizzle came from the kitchen, and Betty moaned.

"Potatoes!" she said in a panic.

"They're fine," Harry replied, reaching for the waistband of Betty's pants.

"They're boiling over!"

Harry ignored all mention of potatoes and slid between Betty's legs, pulling her pants off just far enough for him to thrust into her.

She let out a loud moan and started slapping Harry's shoulders, wanting to get away. He grabbed her arms and pinned her to the couch, leaving her powerless as he thrust harder and faster. Betty closed her eyes and took a deep breath, realizing she had no choice but to let him finish, without debate.

Harry rolled off of her and collapsed onto the couch next to her, his heavy breath drowning out the sound of water sizzling on the stove. He reached over and patted her head.

"The potatoes are boiling over," he said before zipping his pants and leaving the room.

XXII.

Olivia shifted in her seat, turning to look directly at Betty as she let out a deep breath. Before Olivia could even open her mouth to speak, Betty shook her head.

"Times were different. He was my husband. It was to be expected."

The heat was rising in Olivia's face. How could someone say that sexual assault was to be expected? Was consent a new concept?

"I don't care how long ago that was, Harry was an asshole!" Olivia said.

Betty let out a little laugh and shook her head. She closed her eyes for a moment and inhaled slowly before turning to Olivia and nodding.

"They all are sometimes, aren't they?"

Olivia raised an eyebrow and tilted her head, hesitant to agree, but not ready to disagree either.

"You know, it wasn't until the 1970s, I'm not sure the exact year, that a man couldn't force his wife to sleep with him."

"You mean he could rape her," Olivia responded, bluntly.

"Yes, but that word seems so harsh."

Olivia rolled her eyes and tried to wrap her head around something so vile being accepted as normal, and even worse, as expected. Maybe you expected someone to let you down, even expected them to leave you, but to violate you? That was unfathomable to Olivia.

Betty closed her eyes and rubbed her forehead as the women sat in silence for a moment.

“Are men not so careless these days?” Betty asked.

Olivia squinted, unsure of how to answer the question.

“I don’t really know. I have a hard time thinking of things as being so black and white.”

Betty nodded and acknowledged that she had found a more conscientious man in Jack.

Still, it was hard for Olivia to understand how or why women would stay with men who disregarded their feelings, but at the same time, it wasn't too far from her own situation. There was no denying that Olivia could see two drastically different realities of her own. The effortless, albeit boring, life Cole offered her was comforting and safe, but the same could not be said for her escapades with Charlie.

"I guess I knew that Charlie was married, and he wasn't treating his wife well, but it wasn't until I was talking to her in the cafe that I truly understood what I was disrupting," Olivia explained.

Sitting across the table from the woman whose road she had created a fork in, Olivia's leg bounced up and down as she waited to place her order.

“The kids seemed excited to see their dad at work,” Olivia said.

“It’s a rarity. We don’t make it to campus too often. There’s way too much going on at home, and honestly, I think Charlie usually prefers to keep work and home separate," Rachel explained.

The women sat in silence, watching as the children ran their fingers through deep grooves in the wooden booth. Rachel flipped a sticky laminated menu over and scanned the beverages.

"How about fruit smoothies instead of milkshakes, guys?" Rachel asked the kids.

Both groaned, giving her disapproving looks.

"That's Cole's favorite thing to get here," Olivia said, nodding at the kids.

"Really?" they asked in unison.

"Would I lie to you?"

The kids exchanged a look. Tommy squinted, as if trying to detect her lie, and then smiled.

"Can I have a strawberry one?"

"I want banana and blueberry!"

Thank you, Rachel mouthed to Olivia.

The café was empty and quiet, except for the excited chattering of the kids bouncing in their seats, waiting impatiently for their smoothies. Olivia slipped away from the table to place their order. Something told her she owed Rachel at least that much.

"The regular?" Pippa asked from behind the counter.

"No, not today. Can I have two medium coffees, a banana blueberry smoothie, and a strawberry smoothie? You won't believe who I'm here with, Pip."

"A whole crowd, I see," Pippa said as she poured the coffees.

Olivia waited for her to turn around with the coffees, and then motioned to the booth where she had left Charlie's family. Pippa's eyes widened and she tilted her head to the side.

"Is that...?"

"Yeah. It's been an interesting afternoon."

Pippa laughed and shook her head before turning back to finish the smoothies.

"I'll bring them over to you."

Olivia let out a ragged breath and walked back to the booth, interrupting the kids' argument over which one got to choose what they were watching on tv when they got home. Rachel sat quietly, not getting involved in the argument, but giving a knowing look. Most likely by the time they got home, they'd forget all about it.

Olivia handed Rachel her coffee. "I don't know how you take it."

"Thank you. Black is perfect."

"My grandmother used to joke and say, 'I like my coffee like I like my men: hot and black!'" Olivia said with a smile.

Rachel laughed and shifted in her seat.

As if on cue, Pippa came over with the kids' smoothies and a sly smile.

"I think these are for you," she said, placing the drinks on the table in front of them.

"Thank you!" they said in unison before shoving colorful straws into their smoothies.

The café was starting to fill up a little more as college students ran to the counter for a midday caffeine fix. A few looked over at Olivia's table and laughed at the kids who seemed to be racing to finish their smoothies.

"You're going to get stomachaches if you keep drinking that so quickly," Rachel warned.

With the warning from their mother going in one ear and out the other, each of the kids continued to focus on the task at hand: finishing their drink the fastest.

The small talk between Olivia and Rachel could only go so far. Olivia had a secret and way too much guilt to try to have a conversation of any real depth with Rachel, and the anxiety of it all was weighing heavily on her. The sound of slurping was getting louder as the kids got closer to finishing their drinks, and with each slurp, Olivia's heart was beating faster.

"How's Cole?" Rachel asked.

"He's good. Studying a lot lately."

"He seems like a good guy."

"Definitely. I was lucky enough to meet him right at orientation a couple of years ago."

Rachel nodded.

"Does he know about your extracurricular activities with my husband?" Rachel asked in a matter-of-fact tone.

XXIII.

"Did the kids hear her? She wasn't holding back, I see," Betty said.

Olivia looked down at her hands and shifted in her seat before answering.

"No? Maybe? Honestly, I'm not sure."

Olivia was lost in thought. She had no idea if the kids had been listening to her conversation with Rachel, but at the same time, she didn't want to think about it. It was easier to distance herself from any culpability in the trauma an adulterous father was sure to cause if she refused to focus on the victims, the children. She wasn't the one who'd promised someone forever; she wasn't the one who'd brought two beautiful babies into the world and put their sense of normalcy in danger; she wasn't to blame. Some form of that mantra played over and over again in her mind as Olivia worked overtime to assuage her guilt. Of course, that also allowed her to put what she was doing to Cole on the back burner.

"I'm a terrible person," Olivia said quietly as she buried her face in her hands.

Betty reached over and stroked Olivia's back, hoping to bring her some comfort and reassurance. Part of her was afraid that this display of empathy would seem insincere, but she truly did understand. As women, they shouldered the blame in most situations, justified or not. Seeing Olivia struggle with the pain she was all too familiar with herself left Betty with a nagging feeling that she had an opportunity. She had been hesitant to share her perceived shortcomings with Olivia when she first started sharing her story, but she figured there was no time like the present.

"I know you think you're a terrible person, but trust me, I've done worse," Betty said.

Olivia looked over at her, scrunching her face in disbelief.

"I doubt it."

"Well, you can decide for yourself. I told you I had three children, right?" Betty asked.

Olivia nodded, allowing Betty to slip into her story.

"So, it's safe to say I made some mistakes along the way. I had no idea what I was doing, and how I was going to make sure I raised them into three productive members of society," Betty explained.

With more than one child to care for, there was no way for Harry to deny his job wasn't nearly enough for their growing family. By the time Patricia was ten months old, Betty found herself getting up early, not to pack a lunch for Harry, but to curl her hair, pour a cup of coffee, and kiss the kids goodbye on her way out the door. Motherhood offered her a little bit of purpose, but work was an entirely different sense of accomplishment for her. Harry had fallen right in step with the new routine. He stayed with the kids during the day, they ate dinner when Betty got home, and he rushed off to work for the night. Initially, working opposite shifts didn't seem ideal, but it allowed them to live more comfortably. And if Betty was being honest, she didn't mind the space from her husband.

Every night, walking home and being greeted by her adoring children, who had the opportunity to miss her all day, was a breath of fresh air. Joe would run into her arms and Patricia would toddle close behind him. She had believed working would give her that feeling of accomplishment and success that she'd always wanted, but nothing beat the feeling that swept over her as she wrapped her children up in love after a long day away from them.

Without fail, Harry expected that the weekends were days meant for Betty to focus on him and his perceived needs. She, on the other hand, was happy to have two days to stay with her babies and create some great memories. The push and pull between her husband and children dictated her life when she was home. It was physically and emotionally exhausting. No part of her wanted to upset Harry, knowing that nothing good would come of it, but she refused to push her children aside in favor of fulfilling their father's every want.

Of course, there was no way she could always keep him at bay, and in some ways, distance truly did make the heart grow fonder. Without being subjected to his constant pushing and prodding on a nightly basis, Betty started to miss the physical connection they had before life got in the way. It felt more like they were ships passing in the night than a young married couple. That didn't mean there were no opportunities for them to be together. And with Harry's constant attempts to capitalize on the weekends they had together, it didn't take too long for Betty to get pregnant again.

That Wednesday afternoon, walking home from work, knowing she would have to shift right into homemaker mode, Betty was in no rush. Leisurely walking down Main Street, watching children run through the park, yelling after one another and laughing, put a smile on her face. The unexpected face she caught a glimpse of stopped her in her tracks.

"Betty!" a familiar voice yelled.

Her breath caught in her throat as she met his stare. There he was, the man who had tempted her once before, standing right in front of her again.

"Jack! How are you?" she said, pushing through her surprise.

"I'm great now. I was just thinking about you."

"Serendipity. It's a good coincidence, I hope," Betty said.

Jack's smile seemed to widen with every word Betty said, and she couldn't help but reciprocate. There was something undeniably attractive about his broad shoulders, muscular arms, and soft eyes. It didn't take long for the idea of getting home to her children to seem intrusive. Being the responsible mother she was, there was no time for her own desires to be explored.

"I didn't know you were still in town."

"Just got back, actually. I couldn't stay gone for too long," Jack said.

"And you're just taking a walk in the park?" Betty asked.

Jack's head tilted to the side, and he let out a little laugh. "Well, basically. It's a beautiful day, and how often do we really get to be outside?"

"Good point. I'm heading home from work. The kids need me."

"Kids, plural?"

Betty laughed and nodded. "You met Joe, and now I have a little girl, Patricia, as well."

"I bet she's beautiful just like her mother."

"Oh, she's perfect. Her chubby cheeks and perfectly plump little legs make me wish I could spend all of my time cuddling her."

"The second you said you had a daughter I knew she'd be just that amazing."

Betty's cheeks were sore from smiling, but she couldn't seem to stop. Talking to Jack made her genuinely happy, and truly in the moment. It reminded her of simpler times, the ones before she had a husband and kids.

"But really, I should get going. Harry has to get to work, so I'm on baby duty."

"He works nights?" Jack asked, raising his eyebrows.

"We split the time. I work days, he works nights. Then we don't have to pay a sitter," Betty explained.

"If you need some company, I'd be happy to stop by," Jack said before biting his bottom lip.

Betty laughed nervously.

“How presumptuous of you, sir,” Betty said with a wink. Without giving it too much thought, she signaled for Jack to follow her down the road toward her house. As they approached the house, her heart started racing, and she couldn’t help but wonder what she was doing. It felt reckless, dangerous, and ill-advised, but mostly exciting. A change from the monotony of her day-to-day life felt warranted. And there was no reason to believe anything untoward was going to happen when he came back to visit later. The kids would probably be up, needing attention anyway.

Betty stopped short in front of the house and turned to face Jack, who slowly leaned toward her. She could feel the heat rising to her face as she readied herself for a kiss from a man who was little more than a stranger. She glanced up to the windows of her apartment and noticed the curtain ruffle, letting her know someone was looking out.

Jack breezed past her lips with a barely noticeable pause before leaning closer to her ear. “I’ll be back at eight, leave the door open for me,” he said before turning around and walking in the opposite direction.

Trekking up the stairs, expecting her kids to be waiting with their welcome-home hugs, she took a slow, deep breath, and steadied herself for her nightly routine. As usual, Joe was waiting at the door with his arms outstretched, waiting to be swept up into her arms. The anxiety of having been seen dissipated for a moment with her full attention being on her son. The moment she looked beyond Joe, she noticed Harry standing in the entryway to the kitchen, Patricia in one arm, and his focus entirely on Betty.

"Hi," she said as she walked in and greeted her husband with a kiss before taking Patricia from him.

"Took you an awfully long time to get home today," he replied. His suspicion was palpable, but Betty tried to convince herself that she was imagining it. There was no way he thought the reason she was late was another man.

"I know. It's so nice outside today, so I walked home through the park, trying to forget the long workday," she explained, hoping it was a believable excuse.

Harry nodded, although his furrowed brow seemed to be telling a different story, and bent to give Betty a kiss before disappearing into the bedroom to get changed for work.

It seemed to work. Maybe it was Joe who had moved the curtains when she was outside with Jack, or maybe it had just been her imagination, her guilt, but more importantly, she didn't think it had been Harry. Shaking off the nervous energy she had entered the house with, she got started on a quick dinner so they could eat together before Harry set off for work.

"How's spaghetti sound, Joe?"

"With butter?" he asked.

Betty laughed, not sure why he was so averse to using an actual sauce, but she was used to it at this point.

"With butter, buddy."

Cooking pasta had become a science for Betty. Seven minutes to boil the water and ten more after she added the spaghetti. Time was the key to everything.

Seven more minutes to cook.

Thirty-five minutes before Harry left for work.

Two hours before the kids went to bed.

Fourteen days late.

"I don't have time to stick around for crap spaghetti," Harry said, pulling Betty out of her minute-by-minute countdown to nothing and everything at the same time.

"It's almost done," she said, almost as if to apologize for not being able to will the food to cook faster.

"I know. I just have to make a quick stop before I get to the shop, so I need to head out now." Harry put an arm around her waist and pulled her closer as he leaned down, his lips breezing over hers before settling right next to her ear and whispering, "Miss you already," before kissing the kids and heading out the door.

Betty's face whitened as Harry disappeared. He always seemed to know when to turn on the charm to get Betty to second-guess herself. She had to shake it off; there was spaghetti waiting to be buttered, and kids waiting to be fed. It was hard to look away from Joe taking each strand of spaghetti into his mouth like a chubby little bird eating a worm and sucking the butter clear off of every noodle.

"I need more butter, Mommy!" Joe demanded.

"No. You need to eat the spaghetti. Don't you want to grow up to be big and strong?"

Patricia was happily munching on her sauce-covered noodles, making a huge mess for Betty to clean, but she seemed to be eating more of the pasta than her brother. A messy win was still a win. A quick glance over at the clock hanging above the stove made Betty's heart start to beat faster.

6:30 had come faster than expected.

Ninety minutes before her guest arrived.

Thirty-five minutes for baths before bed.

Twenty minutes for bedtime stories.

Fifteen minutes to clean the kitchen.

After Joe finally ate the spaghetti and not just the butter, it was time for Betty to jump into action. Wiping both kids' hands and mouths, she set them free in the living room, giving her time to prepare the bath for them and clear her head. Everything went off without a hitch, she truly did have the timing down to a science, and the kids were snug in their beds waiting for their nightly story by 7:05.

As she was wringing out the cloth she had used to wipe down the stove, there was a quick knock on the door. Right on time. Betty closed her eyes and let out a slow, steady breath before hanging the cloth over the faucet to dry and heading for the door.

"Hi," she said with a shaky voice.

"Hi."

Betty stretched her arm out, welcoming him into the apartment. "Sorry, I was just cleaning up from dinner so things are still a little damp and disheveled."

"Looks great," Jack said, before adding, "I'm not here to see the apartment, though."

Betty could feel heat rush to her cheeks as she looked down at the floor, trying to hide her smile.

"What did you want to see, then?" Betty asked, looking him up and down slowly.

"I'm a sucker for a nice bedroom," Jack said, stepping closer to her.

"I don't know if anything in here is what I'd call 'nice' though."

"Does it have a bed?"

Betty nodded, not taking her eyes off him.

"A door?"

Betty nodded again, this time meeting Jack's step forward with her own. Standing close enough to feel his breath, she bit her bottom lip, refusing to give into the pang of guilt that was rushing through her.

Jack wrapped an arm around her waist, pulling her even closer to him. The heat radiating from his body cocooned her in warmth and desire. There was no turning back. Their tongues danced together as if they were practiced partners falling into an old routine. Betty moaned into his kiss, wanting increasingly more of him with every soft touch. Jack pulled away, but only far enough to speak, "I've been imagining this since that day at the soda fountain."

"Is it everything you imagined?" Betty asked, leaning in and trying to close the gap between them.

He didn't say a word, but the desire in his kiss told her everything she needed to know. With barely a thought, Betty led him to the bedroom, gently kicking the door shut behind them. Jack's hands moved gently along her torso, tracing a line down her side and stopping to make suggestive eye contact when he reached the hem of her shirt and slipped his hand underneath. Betty shivered at the cool touch of his fingers on her warm skin but felt nothing but heat. He lifted her shirt off of her, biting his bottom lip, as he reached behind her to unclasp her bra.

"Even more perfect than I imagined," he whispered before removing her pants.

She closed her eyes and let out a staggered breath as Jack's fingers found their way into her, twisting and teasing with every move.

Fumbling to unbutton Jack's pants, Betty couldn't help but giggle at herself, so overcome with nerves. She was like an awkward and inexperienced teenager all over again.

"Buttons are tough," Jack said with a smile.

Betty's face turned a deeper shade of red than it already was. Of course, her nerves got the best of her at this exact moment. She closed her eyes and took a deep breath before freeing Jack from the confines of his jeans. He pulled his pants down, dropping them on the floor as he pushed Betty back onto the bed and climbed over her.

"You're sure about this, right?" he asked.

She reached up and pulled him down towards her. There was no going back.

XXIV.

The dinging of the "fasten seat belts" sign caught Betty's eye and she shook her head as if to help her move away from the memories she found herself recounting. She used to be so good at keeping track of time, but there was something disorienting about flying, never mind old age, that made her lose her sense of time.

"Any idea how much longer we have, dear?" she asked with a regretful smile.

Olivia looked at her phone. It seemed like time was standing still.

"Maybe two hours? I'm really not sure," she shrugged.

"I don't know why I'm so concerned about time. The clock seems to tick faster when you want to savor a minute and freeze when you want to hurry."

Olivia just laughed. She had never imagined that little old ladies truly did have little nuggets of wisdom to share with unsuspecting strangers. And yet, here she was. There was no question that Betty was right on the mark when it came to time.

It was like the afternoon in the coffee shop. Time had seemed to stand still when Olivia realized Rachel had her and Charles figured out. At that moment, she needed the conversation to end, but of course, life rarely seemed to work out so advantageously.

"Time never seems to be on my side," Olivia explained to Betty.

"Oh, I'm sure that's not true," Betty said with a gentle smile.

Olivia blinked hard and let out a deep breath before jumping back into her story.

"Well, it certainly feels like those moments you need to end last forever. I didn't want to spend another second with Rachel, knowing she must hate me for what I was doing with her husband."

Betty gave a knowing look. Hating the other woman and being unfaithful were things she understood all too well. And without waiting for Betty's response, Olivia picked up where she had left off, sitting in the coffee shop faced with what she had done to Rachel, the wife of the man she was sleeping with, and her children.

Rachel's words echoed in Olivia's mind, and everything around her seemed to slow to a halt. How had she known? Why would she agree to come, never mind bring her children along, when she knew what was happening? Was there a way for Olivia to deny it all and save herself from the humiliation? Realistically, she knew she was caught and had to come to terms with it — face the music, as her mother would say. With every passing second, she thought of another way to try to explain it all away, but nothing felt right. There was no way to justify it, and if Rachel was brazen enough to bring it up in public, denying was pointless. So, instead, she just sat in stunned silence.

Rachel stared back at her, not saying a word. Olivia wasn't sure if that was worse than if she were berating her, because the awkward silence was painful. Knowing this woman was fully aware of the fact that Olivia, someone who had been in her home, playing with her children, and sharing a meal with the family, was so duplicitous was nearly unbearable. There was no avoiding it: she had to come clean.

Olivia looked around the coffee shop, hoping to find a reason to get up from the table and away from the inevitable. She caught Pippa's eye and saw her escape.

"I could use a refill. Want one?" she asked as she stood up.

Rachel looked down at her cup and shook her head.

"Be right back," Olivia said as she took off for the counter, hoping Pippa would have an idea to help her get out of her current predicament.

As she walked between tables and past her fellow students, she could feel her anxiety building. Her heart was racing, and she knew her face was flushed. There was little she could do to fix the situation, but buying herself some time by talking to Pippa wouldn't hurt. Olivia tried feverishly to catch her eye, and without hesitation, Pippa rushed to the counter to meet her.

"What's going on?"

"Pip. She knows," Olivia said.

"It's just your paranoia. There's no way she knows and thinks it's a fun idea to take the kids to hang out with you," Pippa said dismissively.

Olivia shook her head, knowing that was a perfectly logical assumption to make. However, the world isn't always logical.

"No. She flat-out told me. It's not my guilt or imagination."

"Shit. Really? What did she say?"

"She asked if Cole knew about what she called my 'extracurricular activities' with her husband."

Pippa let out a ragged breath and shook her head in disbelief.

"I know. I don't know what I'm supposed to do now. I told her I was just getting a refill. Maybe you can sneak me out the back?"

Olivia let out a little laugh, knowing there was no running away from this situation, even if her fight-or-flight response was leaning heavily towards flight.

"You know you can't just leave. Maybe it won't be so bad. I'm here; I'll keep an eye on you guys. If it looks too heated, I'll come and interrupt with refill offers."

Olivia nodded and looked down at her coffee mug. "I really could use a refill, though."

"Coming right up," Pippa said, grabbing the mug and offering a sympathetic glance. A coffee refill was faster than Olivia would have liked, and before she was truly prepared, she had a fresh cup of coffee in hand and was turned to face the judgment that awaited her.

Every step back towards the table was daunting. Olivia tried her best to concentrate on the steam rising from her drink, but if there was anything less than flames shooting out of the mug it wasn't going to distract her from the doom she felt certain she was walking into. Her own personal green mile may not have a literal executioner waiting for her, but she was absolutely certain that it wasn't going to be pretty. How could this go any other way? If someone slept with Cole, she knew she wouldn't forgive and forget, and it wasn't like they were married. This was worse. Rachel was well within her rights as a wife to be angry, spiteful, and even vengeful. Olivia knew she had to brace herself for the worst-case scenario, but what could that entail? She didn't think it would have any sort of violence, given the children were there, but she wasn't sure of anything beyond that.

She let out one last deep breath as she got closer to the table, and then slipped back into her seat as if nothing had happened. Rachel watched her hem and haw, searching for the words she knew she needed to express her regret, her true desire for atonement.

"Look, Rachel, I know you don't owe me anything, not even understanding."

"No kidding," Rachel said, rolling her eyes.

Olivia winced as if she had expected anything remotely good to happen.

"I am sorry, though. I know it was really shitty. It just kind of happened," Olivia said, looking down at the table like a little kid who had been caught with a hand in the cookie jar.

"Oh, you're sorry? I'd hope so."

Olivia nodded, still doing everything she could to avoid eye contact with Rachel. How could she look the woman she had wronged so badly in the eye?

Some part of Olivia hoped if she looked pathetic enough, Rachel would go easier on her. But she knew she didn't deserve that sort of kindness.

"What can I do? I don't know what's supposed to happen now," Olivia said, almost pleading for some relief from the paralyzing guilt she was feeling.

"I can't tell you that," Rachel said. "I don't know if there's anything that needs to happen here and now."

Olivia furrowed her brow, not sure what to take from that. Was she meant to just go on as if she hadn't just been confronted, or were they going to fight outside? Neither option sounded particularly appealing to her.

"What do you mean?" she asked.

Rachel sighed and glanced over at her kids, peacefully playing together at the next table.

"I mean exactly what I said. Did you really think you were the first student to sleep with my husband?"

Olivia's mouth dropped open and shut again without a sound escaping her lips. She just stared blankly at her with wide, teary eyes.

"Don't cry. I can't stand when the girls cry and try to make me feel bad for them," Rachel said sternly. "I'm the victim here. ME, not you. I was wronged."

With her heart racing faster, Olivia nodded, knowing everything she was being told was the truth. There was no denying that she had done something so reckless, without giving a second thought to the people she might be hurting.

Rachel looked around the café and bit her bottom lip, seeming lost in thought for a moment. When she refocused her attention on Olivia, she smiled.

"I've figured it out."

"Umm, figured what out?"

"How this can be fixed," Rachel said flatly.

Olivia nodded nervously, unsure of what was going to come out of Rachel's mouth. Surely this would go beyond asking her not to sleep with her husband again. That was too easy. The sickeningly sweet smile she flashed showed — what Olivia interpreted as — sinister intentions.

"Ok," Olivia said hesitantly, knowing if she wanted all of the stress and drama to go away, she had little say in the matter.

"Keep sleeping with him."

Olivia's head felt like it was going to explode. She was convinced she had misunderstood something Rachel had said to her. Would a married woman, with two children, honestly encourage the home-wrecking college kid to continue having an affair with her husband?

She let out a little laugh, and looked around, not sure where to focus her attention as she gathered her thoughts and tried to mask her disbelief.

"Not what you expected me to say, huh?" Rachel said.

"No. Not at all. I don't understand. Why would you want me to do that?" Olivia asked with genuine concern in her voice.

Rachel shrugged and ran her fingers through her hair.

XXV.

"I have to admit, I've heard a lot in my years, but that's a first," Betty said, leaning forward and turning to face Olivia.

"Yeah, it's not every day something like that happens."

The two women sat in silence for a few moments, letting the information sink in. The idea that Olivia was being encouraged to sleep with this woman's wife was nearly bewildering. Betty closed her eyes and let out a slow deep sigh, a slight smile creeping across her lips. There was something about knowing that other women made choices that were easy to judge that was comforting to her. She started to believe that maybe Olivia was exactly who she was supposed to share her story with.

The pilot came over the intercom and jolted the women out of their stories and back to reality.

"Ladies and gentlemen, we will be making our descent into Barcelona—El Prat Airport shortly. The temperature there is currently seventy-two degrees and sunny. In the meantime, please just sit back and relax as the flight attendants come around to collect any trash and assist you in any way possible."

"Almost there already?" Betty asked.

"What do you mean 'already'? You've been getting a little antsy over there," Olivia said with a laugh.

Truthfully, between her and Betty's stories, the flight had felt quick to her, too.

"So, I need to know what happened with you and Harry. I know you end up with Jack, but how?" Olivia asked.

"It's a long story," Betty said, leaning back in her seat and letting out a ragged breath.

Without a minute's hesitation, Betty was back to her life before Jack. With her eyes lowered, she bit her bottom lip and focused on her memory of Harry.

Sneaking off into her room with Jack while the baby slept brought Betty back to a simpler time; a time when she and Harry would sneak off to forbidden places to be alone. It was different with Jack though. There was an air of confidence in him that Harry had always lacked, no matter how hard he tried to hide it. His version of being confident was being cruel. There was no way for Betty to be absolutely sure, but she had always chalked his cruelty up to being a reflection of his insecurity. Of course, that belief was based on something her mother had instilled in her from a young age. Most of the time if people were mean, it was about them, not you.

"You're sure he didn't know last time?" Jack asked quietly.

"Of course not," Betty replied, stretching up to kiss Jack's alluring lips.

Jack met her kiss, pushing against Betty and pulling her close to him. The heat between them was instantly palpable. Betty could feel her face flush the second he wrapped an arm around her waist and pulled her in.

"I've been thinking about this since the minute I left you last," Jack whispered.

"Me too," Betty breathed into his chest.

Betty pulled away and guided Jack to the bed. As he pulled himself backward, never taking his eyes off of the forbidden woman he was quickly falling in love with, Betty reached to unfasten his pants before joining him on the bed. There was no turning back and little time to waste. Betty straddled Jack leaving his hips gyrating and all of him longing for penetration. When he was no longer able to wait, Jack rolled quickly, positioning Betty onto the bed.

"Oh! Someone's impatient," she laughed.

Without a word, Jack reached down and positioned himself before thrusting forward. Both of them were lost in the throes of passion, not wanting the night to end, when Betty heard a soft creak. At the moment, she told herself it was the bed, but when a thin stream of light hit her face she knew. Harry was home.

"Get off of me!" Betty yelled in the softest voice she could manage.

"What's wrong? Did I hurt you?" Jack asked.

"Harry is home," she said slowly.

Careful not to make another sound, Jack moved off of Betty and pulled his clothes on. If there was one useful skill he had learned in the military, it was using swift and silent movement. Betty needed him to leave without being heard or seen, and he was more than capable of doing that. She opened the window behind her bed and motioned for Jack to climb out.

"You remember you're not on the first floor, right?" he asked nervously.

"Yes. There's lattice on the side of the building, and then wooden crates are stacked up a few feet below that."

"A woman who knows how to do reconnaissance, I like it," Jack said, leaning in for one last kiss before scurrying down the side of the house.

Betty laid back in bed, pulling the covers over herself and curling up in a sleeping position. Harry's heavy footsteps moved throughout the apartment for what felt like an eternity. Each door creaked open and clicked shut a few seconds later. She was sure he was checking on the children, unless he was looking for her. Betty shook her head, trying to rid herself of the idea that Harry had the slightest idea that she hadn't been alone with the kids all night.

"There you are," Harry whispered, crawling into bed with Betty.

"Where else would I be?"

"Sometimes you're in with the kids."

"It's been a long day with them, so I was more than ready for bed."

"I've been ready for you all day," Harry said, pulling her close to him.

Betty cringed at his touch. If she wasn't going to be spending the night with Jack, she'd just as soon be sleeping.

"You smell like booze, again. I thought you were at work," she said.

Harry let out a frustrated grunt. "Of course I was at work. Why are you such a bitch?"

"Get off of me!" Betty yelled, pushing her full weight into Harry, believing that would let him know she wasn't in the mood for his antics. However, she wasn't expecting the violence she was met with in return.

"What did you say to me?" Harry growled and pushed himself onto her, tearing her shirt from her body as he pinned her to the bed.

For the rest of the night, Betty was captive in her own bedroom, and even her pleas to allow her to check on the children went unnoticed. Harry was in an angry, frantic trance and he didn't seem like he'd let anything stop him.

"Do you think I'm an idiot?" he blurted out. "I know there was a man here when I got home," he said flatly.

"No. There wasn't. I don't know why you would think that. Please just stop this!" Betty pleaded with her husband. Tears stained her face and her breathing was ragged, but none of that was slowing Harry down.

"I heard him," Harry asserted.

"It was probably the TV."

"I heard you too," Harry said, shaking his head.

Betty had no response. Her head fell, knowing she was caught and in some karmic way, this was her punishment. That didn't mean she had no way forward though.

The "fasten seat belt" signs in the plane came on with a ding before the pilot came over the speaker again.

"Ladies and gentlemen, we have put the "fasten seat belt" signs on again as we are in our final descent into Barcelona. We are waiting for the all clear from the tower before landing."

"Betty, please tell me you called the police this time," Olivia said with a sense of urgency and panic in her voice.

Betty just shook her head.

"Why not?" Olivia said, holding back tears for this woman she had only met a few hours ago.

"There are limits to what the legal system can do. And remember, we were married."

With that, Olivia found herself angry and lost in thought. She couldn't help but wonder what Betty meant when she said there were limits to the law. It was hard to pinpoint the type of shortcomings the system had for a white woman, but then it hit her.

"Did you...?"

"Did I what, dear?"

"Take care of Harry?"

"For far too long, yes. And then, one day he met Jack."

Olivia's eyes widened and her breath quickened. She started to think it was possible that she was just too interested in true crime shows and saw everything as a possible murder, but her alarm bells were going off. Did this sweet old woman have her husband killed? By her lover? Did she help? The questions were endless.

"What happened to Harry, I can't say," Betty said matter-of-factly.

"Because..." Olivia asked, hoping for a little elaboration.

"Because I don't know. Not exactly, anyway," Betty said.

"How could you not know?"

"Not every question needs answers."

Olivia let out a frustrated sigh. How was it possible that she had spent the entire flight hanging on this woman's every word, only to be left without answers?

"Meeting Jack was the answer I had been looking for," Betty explained. "He offered a solution to all my problems. One day, he ran into Harry while he was out for a walk, and that was all he ever told me. It was all I needed to know when Harry didn't come home for a while. Jack fixed it."

The mechanical grinding of the plane's landing gear being lowered took Betty by surprise. Flying was peaceful; landing was terrifying.

"You want some gum?" Olivia asked, popping a piece of minty relief into her mouth.

"No thank you, it'll stick to my dentures," Betty responded while swallowing hard, trying to ease the pressure on her ears.

The plane bounced onto the runway, jostling the women in their seats before pinning them back to the seats as the plane raced to a stop. When the plane finally stopped and attached to the gate, a few random passengers were clapping for a safe landing, while everyone else bustled about the cabin, reaching for their belongings in the overhead compartments.

"Welcome to Barcelona, ladies and gentlemen. Your luggage will be in carousel four. On behalf of the entire crew, we hope you enjoy your stay in Barcelona, and thank you for flying with us today," the captain announced to mostly uninterested passengers, eager to get their vacations started.

XXVI.

Row by row, people shuffled forward, squeezing overstuffed carry-on bags down the aisle to the exit. Betty seemed unfazed by the arrival, but she smiled and looked up, thinking, *We made it Jack,* before realizing that Olivia was waiting to help her get her bag.

"Here you go. You only had one, right?" she asked.

"Oh yes, just the one. Thank you, dear," Betty replied.

Olivia placed Betty's bag on the floor in front of her, passing her the handle so she could pull it along behind her. Once Betty started for the exit, Olivia grabbed her own bag and followed her into the airport. It was eerily silent at the gate, but there were plenty of people marching along like ants on a mission, stepping onto moving sidewalks, looking for customs, and hoping their luggage hadn't been lost in transit.

As the women approached the luggage carousel, they realized this was probably going to be the last time they saw each other. For Olivia, having a goodbye when all she wanted to do was be alone was unexpectedly emotional. Somehow this elderly woman had made her way into her heart in a matter of hours. Betty, too, was more emotional than she had anticipated. She had said big goodbyes before, but she always planned for them. Olivia had come out of nowhere and stolen her heart.

"I'm so glad I got to meet you, Betty," Olivia said as she grabbed her luggage before it passed by her.

"The pleasure is all mine, sweetie," Betty said, reaching out for a hug.

As she pulled away from Betty, Olivia switched her phone off of airplane mode just in time to get a text from a familiar number.

Turn around.

A smile formed across Olivia's face. She'd known he'd find her here. They had always talked about a quick escape from reality. He'd thought Barcelona would be perfect. That was why she'd chosen to go there now. She took a deep breath, ran her fingers through her hair, and turned around slowly.

The person standing there was definitely familiar, but beyond unexpected.

"Wha-what are you doing here?" Olivia stammered.

"Sucks to be blindsided, huh?"

Courtney Kuketz

Acknowledgments

Thanks to: my family and friends for all the support you've thrown behind my writing; Brady Weldon for designing the amazing cover art; my writing group at Bardsy for helping me stay focused on writing while also embracing my awkwardness; my editor, Kenneth Zink, for helping me restructure some imperfections. Without them, this novel would still be an idea floating around my mind.

www.ingramcontent.com/pod-product-compliance
Lightning Source LLC
Chambersburg PA
CBHW060544310726
48982CB00009B/1372/J

* 9 7 9 8 2 1 8 2 2 9 2 5 2 *